Leaving Memphis

Leaving Memphis

First of a trilogy

by

Joy Phillips Routt

Table of Contents

Chapter 1 1

Chapter 2 37

Chapter 3 53

Chapter 4 68

Chapter 5 81

Chapter 6 99

Chapter 7 113

Chapter 8 129

Chapter 9 138

Chapter 10 149

Chapter 11 170

Chapter 12 184

Chapter 13 208

Chapter 14 212

Chapter 15 216

Chapter 16 219

Chapter 17 226

Chapter 18 236

Chapter 19 243

Chapter 20 251

Chapter 21 255

Chapter 22 260

Chapter 23 292

Chapter 1

"Your wish is my command. Be there in a few."

He had said those words to her for as long as he could remember. It was kind of their thing.

Winston smiled when he heard Nicole blowing kisses through his iPhone. He punched the off button, then turned into the liquor store parking lot. His wife wanted a specific brand of Chardonnay for tonight's dinner and he was tasked to fetch it.

Winston didn't mind. He had been married to his breathtaking beauty for almost thirty years. Nicole looked more like a twenty something super model, than a forty-eight-year-old housewife.

She was genius brilliant, caring, funny, fun, and had a killer body. All his friends envied him. He smiled, for he also knew he was going to get lucky tonight.

He reached to turn off his powerful sound system he had installed in his new C300 Mercedes-Benz. Just as his hand touched the off button, Bruce Springsteen's "Secret Garden" began to play, instead he turned the volume up. This was Nicole's favorite song. The magical saxophone blared through the speakers. He leaned his head back, closed his eyes and immersed himself into the haunting sound of the horn.

Suddenly, a shot crashed through the front tinted window, smashing into the side of his head.

A LITTLE MORE THAN A YEAR AGO HER HUSBAND WAS SHOT DEAD.

Shot in a parking lot of a liquor store in Memphis. Ten minutes before, they had been laughing together on their cells. Then, just like that he was gone, no more, and it was her fault.

Her fault he was in that part of town at that liquor store. She had asked him to pick up a certain Chardonnay she had read about in a magazine sold only at the South Memphis location. Her fault. Those two words crowded her mind day in and day out, month after month, driving her to the black edge.

Finally, out of desperation, she sold their home, left her beloved Memphis and moved to New York City to be near their daughter.

Still, the black hole of depression followed her. Each day it became darker and deeper. Nothing was good. Especially, on days like this day when she was summoned to her New York attorney's offices. Like all the times before, she left their office with silent tears flowing.

"Damnit."

2

Nicole wiped the back of her long slender fingers across her face and leaned against the wall.

At that moment, two well-dressed men exited the university admission offices housed across the hall from her attorneys. She lowered her head and began fumbling through her purse, hoping they wouldn't see her falling apart.

The two men were engaged in an intense conversation and didn't seem to notice. They walked pass her toward the elevators. When they entered, and the door closed, she breathed a sigh of relief. Slowly, she walked to the elevators, and punched the down button.

As she descended, her thoughts went to the reason she was at her attorney's office. Since she had moved to New York, Nicole met with them at least twice a month. With her husband's death, she became sole owner of the highly successful Winn's Sports Enterprise. Her older brother Jim ran the day to day operations that were headquartered in Memphis. Jim had been President of the company for many years, and now, he was the CEO of the conglomerate.

It was such a godsend that her brother was there to run the company. She had no idea what she would have done without him, for she had very little knowledge of the day to day operations. That was Winston's kingdom, and she was in charge of their daughter, Madison and the home.

She was in the process of making her brother a partner. However, until that happened, Jim would send papers to their New York attorney's office for her to sign.

Today, when she was finished, her attorney, placed another piece of paper on the desk.

"Before you leave you need to sign this tax form."

"What is it?"

"It is a form from the Federal Government, stating you are officially considered a single person, and will be taxed as such."

"Single?"

"I know, I know, but it's the law. Just sign it, and I will take care of the rest."

Raymond handed her a pen and motions her toward the legal document. She almost couldn't see the line to sign for the swelling tears. Quickly, she scribbled her name, stood up to grab her coat and purse. Raymond tried to help her with her coat, but she pulled away. Instead he took her hand and began patting it.

"If you need anything, all you have to do is call. Just call sweetheart, and I will take care of everything. You needn't worry about anything."

Nicole smiled, and pulled her hand away, as she inched toward the door.

"Thank you, Raymond."

Once in the hall, she clinched her teeth and said to herself.

"What I need, you, patronizing son of a bitch, is for my husband to come back to me, and I am not single, not single."

She blew her nose.

"I hate this, hate it. I just want to go home. Home, what a joke. Home is Memphis, where my life is... was... back when I had a life."

At that moment, the elevator stopped on the tenth floor. As the door opened, three young men entered. Nicole had noticed them before. They were always full of boyish pranks and laughter. She assumed they were students from the university located in the building.

Many times, she had seen young men and women gather in the hallways or on the elevators. Backpacks on backs, books in hands. It was a good thing. Well, maybe not today, for the trio were speaking in their native Russian language, Turkic.

They were talking about a female in one of their classes and what they wanted to do to her. The longer they spoke the cruder their language became. Little did they know Nicole understood every word they uttered.

Times like this, she wished she didn't have her special gift. But she did, so when the elevator stopped at the lobby, Nicole turned to the three and spoke in their native tongue.

"You boys might want to reconsider, for that is a crime in this country. Have a nice day."

She walked out of the elevator and heard them scream with laughter when the door closed. She smiled to herself. Maybe that will teach them to be more careful about what they say in public.

Every time she had appointments with her attorney, she would watch the students come and go through the lobby. Most of them were of different cultures. She loved to watch the diversity represented in this building, marveling at what a white bread world she had lived in Memphis.

Except for the amazing pro athletes with the Grizzles basketball team and the University of Memphis sports teams, and of course The University of Tennessee Vols, she occasionally met at fundraiser parties, Nicole wasn't around many other cultures hardly at all.

Winston and his best friend Tennessee Senator Jackson Freeman were regulars at the Big Orange games. While she loved the game of football, she rarely attended the games. She let that be their guy thing while she opted to watch games on TV.

The two men played on the Volunteer football team during collage and afterward were huge donors of the UT sports department. They were VIP and got to know all the players well. Of course, with Winn Sports Enterprise it was their business to be familiar with all the players, and most of the players in this area of the country were black. However, Nicole was not that involved with the business, so she rarely socialized with them. Winston didn't include her in the business operations much. She raised Madison, and he took care of the business. A very southern approach to married life back then.

Also, in Memphis, it was more of an economic choice than anything else. They had been blessed with incredible financial success, which in-turn afforded them a fabulous lifestyle filled with choices. However, since Winston's death, regardless of the wealth, all that fabulousness had turned to dust in her mind.

Nicole pulled her hood over her head and walked out the revolving door into the freezing rain, sleet, and snow, as the whirling wind whipped through her tall slender body. It didn't take long for her smile to fade, replaced with the usual darkness. Now days, darkness was pretty much all she knew. Pretending to be okay was wearing her down.

There was a time when she had been truly happy. A time when she had been warm.

"God, I hate this place, why did I move here."

Tears flowed. Nicole stopped in front of a store window to wipe her tears and readjust her scarf. She tightened it around her neck and flipped the hood up once again.

As she turned, she noticed the three boys from the elevator walking down the sidewalk. They were still laughing, then suddenly they weren't. With-in seconds, the trio stood like stone faced soldiers, as a black unmarked van with dark tinted windows pulled up near them. The van's automatic doors opened and the three marched in, then the van sped away.

She stared at the vehicle as it disappeared into traffic. Nicole assumed the boys were being shuttled to student housing. It struck her how quickly they went from smart ass fun-loving boys to what looked like scared little soldiers. She wondered what their story was. She wondered why the van was unmarked.

At that moment, a pedestrian bumped into her, causing her to stumble. Fortunately, she caught herself.

"God, please don't let me fall. My daughter will freak if I break something."

Twenty blocks later she rounded the corner onto Bleaker Street to her apartment building. Minutes later, she shut the door to her fourth-floor apartment, turned her locks and set the chain.

"At last."

Quickly, Nicole skimmed out of her wet clothes, and soaked shoes. She grabbed her warmest socks, sweater, and sweats, dried her hair and headed to her tiny kitchen to make a cup of hot tea.

Another new thing, for in the South iced tea was the drink of choice. But here in New York it was hot tea.

She smiled as she remembered the very first time, she had ordered tea in a New York restaurant, expecting it to be a nice large glass of the iced drink, instead the waitress plopped down a cup of hot water with a tea bag beside it. She still had not gotten used to the hot tea taste but adding a bit of bourbon helped. Just as she capped off the teacup, her cell phone rang. It was her daughter, Madison.

"Hi sweetie, yes, I am home. No, I promise I won't be going out again. Yes, I am all locked up, the dead bolts and chains are in place."

Nicole took a sip of her hot toddy.

"How was your day sweetheart? Oh, that's all right, I will talk to you in the morning. Okay, if it snows too much I won't go out, I promise. Yes, sweetie you guys have a nice evening. Tell Zack hi. Love you both."

Nic crossed over to the sink, poured the rest of her doctored tea down the drain. She then reached in her cabinet for the bottle of re-corked Merlot. She took out a large wine glass, filling it to the rim, grabbed a box of crackers and headed for the living room.

Once settled on her couch, she picked up the remote, turned on the TV, only to mute it. Since she had moved to New York, she almost always had the television on, yet ninety percent of the time it was on mute, another new thing in her life. Just one of the many new things in her life that had changed so drastically over the past year.

As she sipped her wine, Nic thought of her daughter. She was the reason for the move here. Madison had been living in the city since graduating from Tulane.

What an awesome grown up she turned out to be. She had made it past the angst of teenage years, and the struggles of young adulthood. They had successfully gotten beyond the time honored "anger at mom" stage daughters seem to go through. At least, the moms she knew had to walk that path. Today, their relationship was great. However, now days, Madison spent too much time worrying about her. Nicole knew it was because of what happened to Winston.

Today her daughter was a successful career woman. Just last month, she was promoted to vice president of her division where she worked, quite a coup for a twenty-nine-year-old woman in the New York business world. She oversaw all the PR events within the thirty-two upscale stores spread throughout the world. Three years ago, she married Zack, who was successful in his own right.

They have a great apartment, super friends, and a cute little Yorkie named Tank. Nicole smiled as she thought of her adorable grand-puppy. What fun she was having playing with him. Of course, now that it was snowing no way would her daughter allow an outing tomorrow. She could just hear Madison.

"Are you kidding mom, with all the snow and ice? You might fall. Do you want to give me a heart attack?"

Back when Nic lived in Memphis, her daughter would call on her way to work. Back then, they would talk about things, sometimes important things, sometimes silly things. She

10

remembered how she thought about living closer to her only child, about being able to help her, but now that she was here, things were different.

Nic went back to the kitchen for a refill, removed a chunk of cheese from the refrigerator, shoved the door shut with her hip and returned to the couch. As she covered her feet with the throw her thoughts went back to her daughter. How the tables had turned over the past year. Now Madison was the one worrying. Living in the same city had placed an extra burden on her. How unrealistic she had been, thinking that moving to New York was the answer.

There was no answer except for her husband to be alive again. That was the only thing that would make things right.

She took a large gulp of wine and started back to the kitchen of another re-fill. She stopped and picked up her iPhone to text Madison a good night message.

"I am going to bed and watch TV."

That was a lie.

After getting a nightly text back from her daughter, Nicole continued to the kitchen.

"Just one more, just tonight, that's it."

Knowing full well she had said the same thing to herself almost every night for a year. Instead of the bedroom she settled back onto the couch. Tears started flowing as they had done for so many nights before in this past year.

Nic popped in one of her old home movies. That was another thing she promised herself to stopped doing. Yet, she knew she would take one more stroll down memory lane. This DVD was one of her husband and Madison when she was just a child.

Watching Christmas through the eyes of a five-year-old was incredible. Full of innocence and wonder, so eager to believe.

As the camera rotated around to Winn, Nic leaned closer. He was breathtakingly handsome. She watched her husband pick up their daughter and swing her high. They went around and round, laughing hard. So much love, so much fun, so long ago.

Nicole grabbed the remote and punched hard at the off button. She had to stop this. A life that will never be again. Madison was grown, and Winn was gone.

Another drink of Merlot brought more memories forward.

It had been over a year since that afternoon when the police came to the door. She thought it was Winn playing around, teasing her by ringing the doorbell. She almost unbuttoned her blouse before opening the door just to tease him back. Thank goodness she didn't, for it certainly wasn't Winston.

He had called her on his cell to get the name of the Chardonnay she wanted. Before he hung up, the last thing he said to her,

"Your wish is my command. Be there in a few."

He laughed and hung up.

That was it, the very last words he would ever say to her. Damn it, why hadn't she just gotten off her lazy ass and gone to the liquor store herself. Or better yet, they had plenty of wine at home. Why hadn't she just told him to come on home? If she had, she would be back in Memphis in the beautiful home, with her wonderful husband, having fun, being with friends, being together.

She had texted him earlier that day to ask him if he would stop by the liquor store for a Chardonnay she had read about. She just didn't want to get out. If she had he would not have been in that parking lot. He would not have been shot. He wouldn't have died. Damn it to hell, it was not fair, and it was all her fault.

Nic put down her wine glass and grabbed the top of her head, pressing hard with both hands. She had to stop thinking about it. Every time she did for any length of time, the air left her lungs. In fact, one of the main reasons she sold their home in Memphis and moved to New York was because she could no longer breathe.

Day after day, time after time, place after familiar place sucked the air from her. Despite everyone telling her she should wait a year before making big decisions, she felt she had no choice but to leave Memphis.

Yet, even after a year she still had no clue how to live without him. Winn was her one and only. They had started dating when she was a freshman in high school. She had never been with anyone else. It was always him.

The room faded from her mind as Nicole's thoughts went to when she first met Winn. She remembered that night like it was yesterday.

She recalled her dad's exact words.

"Nic, you know your mother and I are not going to let you stay at home alone, so stop pouting and get dressed. It will be fun, you'll see, plus it's your brother's first game. He needs our support."

Little did she know how much that night would change her life. It was the first time she had ever laid eyes on Winston Roberts. She watched him race down he football field like he was some kind of god.

After the game her brother Jim introduced Winston, the star quarterback, to their dad.

"Nice to meet you sir, and please call me Winn. That is what I go by."

Jim, of course completely ignored her but her dad didn't.

"Winston, excuse me, Winn, this is Jim's little sister, Nicole. This is her first football game."

How red hot her face felt, as she stammered out a pathetic "hi". He smiled and said hello. That was it. That was all it took. She was changed forever. Of course, she was too young to even realize what was happening. She just knew it felt all tingly inside.

The year before she had started her period and all she had gotten from that was pain and embarrassment. Never had her body felt anything like this. It was crazy scary, but she kinda liked it.

At that time, she was in the eighth grade… eighth grade for Christ sake, and he was the high school football star. No way was she going to have a chance with him. So, she admired him from afar. Learned everything there was to know about Winn, about the sport he played.

She learned about tackles, quarterbacks, linebackers, wide receivers, 53 men roster, touchdowns, etc. etc. She studied charts, and interpretations, and soon became an expert. It didn't take long for her to fall in love with the game of football. She talked her dad into taking her to all the games. It became a daddy daughter thing. Of course, he didn't know the real reason.

Her mom began helping at the food stand with the other moms, and dad loved the idea of his daughter doing something with him that wasn't "girly". They forged a real relationship because of football… because of Winston.

Nicole became an expert in all things football. She knew the plays, the statics, everything. Word got out. She would never forget the day the coach approached her in the school hallway.

"Nicole, could you meet me in Principle Spencer's office after your class, we would like to speak with you."

Somehow, she squeaked out, "Yes sir."

It didn't matter what class she was in because for the next forty minutes, she heard nothing, learned nothing.

The many scenarios of what was going to happen in the Principal's office was terrifying. Her imagination ran amuck. She just knew they were going to out her for being a stalker. Word would spread and her already miserable geeky life would get worse. By the time she managed to walk into the administration office, her wobbly legs barely carried her.

Her dad was there as well. God, how bad could this be? She was mortified. Tears filled her eyes. It was then her dad spoke up.

"Nicole, sweetie, nothing is wrong. Everything is okay, I promise."
He reached for her hand and squeeze it.

"Here sit down next to me and let Coach Johnson explain."

Turns out the coach wanted her to do the statistics for each game. Seems her brother Jim had taken some of the sheets of paper she had compiled concerning the football stats and shown them to Coach Johnson. Her brother, of all people, maybe he wasn't such a monster after all.

So, for the rest of her school career she complied the statistics for the football team, and just like that, she became a member of the most exclusive club in school. She hung with the cool kids. More importantly, she hung around Winn. By the end of her freshman year, they had started dating. Of course, that bought forth a whole new set of age difference issue with her parents. So many arguments, so many tears, but somehow, they made it. Nicole couldn't help but smile as she remembered how hard Winn had fought for them. He was always respectful to her parents, but he intended for them to be together. By the time he was a senior in college, both sets of parents finally accepted them as a couple.

It was a good thing, because near the end of her freshman year at The University of Tennessee, she became pregnant. Soon they were married, and the rest is history.

Thirty years later, here she was, alone. She was no longer in Memphis with Winn, with their friends, no more laughing, having fun. Now she was alone in New York City. And all because she wanted some damn Chardonnay. It was her fault he went to that place. Since that day, she couldn't look at a glass of Chardonnay let alone drink one. If only she could only go back and change things. Nicole poured the last of the Merlot and opened a new bottle. She thought of the day Winn was shot. After the police came to her door everything happened so quickly, and yet everything seemed to slow to a crawl.

Madison and Zack flew down and along with her brother Jim's help, made the arrangements. What would she have done without them? They did everything.

As she took another sip of wine, her thoughts drifted to her years with Winn. He pretty much did everything for her all their lives. He was such a wonderful provider. She wanted for nothing. He was her rock.

Now she walked on quicksand. Nothing was safe, nothing was good.

Much later in the evening, and far too many glasses of wine, black thoughts crowded her soul. Her self-hate was all consuming. She was tired, beat down. There was no fight left. She just couldn't do it anymore.

"Damn it, stop!"

Nicole got up from the couch, somehow stumbled to the kitchen and poured a full glass, one more time. She could hardly walk. She had not moved to New York to become a drunk, yet, here she was again, just as she had been many nights before, hardly able to make it to the bathroom.

What a burden she had become, for her daughter. She reached into the medicine cabinet for an aspirin bottle. Instead, her shaky hand moved over to the prescription bottle given to her the day of Winston's funeral. The doctor told her the pills would take the edge off. She had taken just one and it made her loopy, so she had not taken anymore. She should have tossed them, but she hadn't. Now, as her fingers wrapped around the bottle, her heart raced. She unscrewed the top and poured one pill into the palm of her trembling hand. Nicole just stared at it for a moment, frozen. She placed the pill on her tongue and took a swallow of wine.

Slowly she picked up another pill and swallowed it. Tears streamed down her cheeks. She put the wine glass on the vanity and poured the rest of the pills into her hand. The mounting tears made it hard for her to see or breathe.

"I just want the pain to stop. I don't want to see that look in my daughter's eyes anymore. I am such a burden to her. She would be so much better off."

Nicole reached for her glass but knocked it off. She tried to grab it, only to spill the hand full of pills as the crystal crashed onto the floor.

Glass shattered into pieces, wine spilled everywhere. Nicole dropped to her hands and knees trying to gather up the wine-soaked pills. A piece of glass cut into her palm.

"Shit."

She was bleeding.

Suddenly, out of nowhere, Nicole was staring at her favorite black and white framed photo, the one of her and Winston on the beach in Destin, Florida. She always kept it on her nightstand next to her bed, always.

"How did it get down here on the floor? I don't understand. I don't remember."

She began to cry uncontrollably. Her whole body shook.

"Oh God, what have I done? Oh God, God."

She crawled to the toilet and stuck her fingers down her throat again and again until she up chucked everything.

Then very slowly, got up and held onto the walls as she stumbled back to the kitchen. She retrieved a dustpan and brush. Just as slowly she returned to the bathroom and once again on her knees swept up the broken glass and wine-soaked pills. She tossed them into the garbage can.

Nicole was shaken to the core. How could she have done this? How could she? She washed out her mouth over and over. She had seen in the movies that people who have overdosed, are taken to the shower. So, she spent the next thirty minutes standing underneath the flow of water on her body, until the water turned cold. She stepped out of the shower and wrapped a towel around her shaking body. Afterwards, she made her way to the bedroom. She placed the photo on the nightstand back where it belonged. Then with all her efforts left, she paced back and forth around her bedroom over and over again until she could pace no more. Finally, she pulled back the covers and crawled into bed.

Her body shook wildly, her teeth shattered, while tears poured.

"Dear God, what have I done? How could I? Oh God, Winston please help me."

Nicole kept the light on beside her bed, afraid to be in the dark. What if part of the pills were already in her system? She thought about how much wine she had consumed.

"What if I can't wake up?"

Too afraid to close her eyes, she cried hard, she cried deep into the center of her soul. Finally, her body slowed the shaking, and sleep won out. It was past noon the next day before she opened her eyes. It took only moments for her to remember what happened last night.

"Shit."

Guilt of what she had almost done, consumed her. Her head hammered, her throat was on fire, and her stomach rumbled violently. She raced to the bathroom. Finally, her body settled enough to take another shower.

Once finished, she searched for the bottle of Excedrin. She had to have them to survive. She grabbed a couple and went into the kitchen. Reaching way back into the shelf in the refrigerator she retrieved a Diet Pepsi. Her hands shook as she popped the top and guzzled the carbonated beverage. It was another one of her guilty pleasures she hid from her daughter. She would just go on and on about how bad the sodas were for her.

Nic grabbed a nutri-biscuit and headed to her desk in her living room. Today would be different, it had to be.

She was still in shock about what she had almost done. She would never go there again, ever! How could she allow herself to do such a thing? How could she? She had to do something today. She could not continue like this. Guilt overwhelmed her. Today she would start over, she had to. Nicole sat at her desk and pulled out a legal pad from the drawer. Her hands shook wildly as she tried to jot down things she wanted to accomplish, but nothing came.

"Shit, Shit Shit!"

She began making angry circles on the page, then ripped the sheets from the pad, wadded and threw them across the room as she began to scream at the top of her lungs. She screamed until she could no more. She leaned back and took a long deep breath. She could hardly swallow.

After a few minutes, Nic picked up the legal pad again, and finally, wrote one word… Language.

As she wrote, her thoughts went back to when she was in the third grade. The Principle had called her parents for an after-school meeting. She didn't remember it, but her parents had told the story over and over again until she felt like she did.

"With your permission, we would like to test Nicole's intelligence. We would like to establish her I. Q."

Seeing the confused look on their faces, Principle Spencer quickly stated.

"You see, we think she is exceptionally intelligent. Once we establish her number, we can proceed with a schedule for her."

Dr. Jane Spencer, rose from behind here desk, walked around to the front and leaned against it.

"There are a number of programs available for her, however, we can't apply for them without first establishing her I. Q. Plus, we have a few questions for you as her parents, just to establish her background."

Several questions were asked about the family history, concerning any language connections.

"Is there anyone in your family especially adapted at different languages?"
Charlene Phillips answered.

"I did fairly well in my Spanish class, but nothing special, and I am not aware of any abilities my daughter might have. Surely I would know."

"There is no reason you should. We stumbled on this by accident. Her Spanish teachers overheard Nicole on the playground. One of the yardmen asked a co-worker where the hose was. They were speaking to each other in Spanish. Señor Walker stated that when the co-worker said he didn't know, Nicole answered in Spanish. She told them where the hose was located."

Mrs. Spencer took a deep breath and began again.

"Since there was no indication on her application forms that she was fluid in Spanish, quite frankly we were curious as to why that information was not in her files."

Mrs. Spencer took another deep breath and continued.

"You see, we are required by law to report any unusual phenomenon's concerning our minor students."

The Principle let that sink in and began again.

"We, of course, know you both, know Nicole so instead of reporting to the authorities, we investigated. Mrs. Walker followed her gut. She is multi-lingual and was able to speak different dialects to Nicole. Each time your daughter answered in whatever language Mrs. Walker spoke. Since no one else was around to hear what was being said, there was no interruption of the classes."

Charlene Phillips was still reeling over the innuendoes of what Mrs. Spencer had said earlier. The very fact that someone was questioning her legal rights to her daughter made it hard to hear anything else.

"After twenty-one hours of labor, trust me, I know who my child is. Check with the Baptist East Maternity Ward if you need. I think we are done here."

She rose from her seat and preceded to the door.

"Where is my daughter?"

Just as any other mother tiger, believing her young was being threatened, she gave her husband the death stare.

"William?"

Confused he rose to follow his wife.

"Please, Mr. And Mrs. Phillips, we are on your side. Just hear me out. Everything is okay, I just needed you to know what had taken place. Our protocols have to be followed."

The Principle motioned for them to return to their seats.

"Please."

William and Charlene reluctantly sat back down.

"We have established that she has an extraordinary gift, one like no other I have ever encountered. We would like to accelerate her classes. There are government programs galore for gifted children. As I said before, we need to establish her I. Q. number. With that we can create a government sponsored program to fit her."

After about an hour, her parents were on board. She took the test the following week and established her number to be one hundred sixty, same as Einstein's. Evidently that was a big deal because suddenly she had a different class schedule. She had advance language classes and an innovative computer program class.

The school bought their first Osborne microcomputer just for Nicole's use. The classes were administered in the principal's conference room. Of course, this made her different from the other kids. That was the last thing she wanted.

What few friends she had started treating her differently, started backing away. From the third grade on, things were difficult. She was the school nerd, the geek, the freak. Finally, in the fifth grade a new girl named Mimi transferred to her school. Turns out Mimi had a high I. Q. as well. They became fast friends. Together they made their way through the mine fields of grade school toward the war zone called high school. They were still considered the nerds, still bullied, until the day the coach asked her to be part of the football organization.

That day was also the first time in her life she ever asserted herself.

"I would like my best friend Mimi to do this with me."

To her surprise, they said yes. And that was that. Within a twenty-four-hour span, she and Mimi went from being harassed to becoming members of the popular crowd. It was amazing and equally shameful how much easier their lives became. How great school was after that. So much fun, so much better. That is, until Winston went to college. She didn't think she would survive being away from him. One day, out of frustration, one of her advisors suggested.

"If you want to be with him, then accelerate your classes. Your IQ numbers state you are a major genius, so go be one!"

And so, she did. She figured out how to accelerate her classes. By the end of her junior year she was done. She skipped the senior year. She graduated and was a freshman at the University of Tennessee with Winston by the time she was barely seventeen. It was the most wonderful time of her life. She was in college. She was with Winn.

Nicole was learning on a totally different level. She attended two different language classes her freshman year, unheard of; Spanish and French. The spoken words of the world were easy for her yet learning to read and write the different languages was more of a challenge. She also excelled in her computer classes. She had decided she wanted to join the United Nations when she graduated. She interviewed with a representative from the U. N. on Career Day. The man's name was Mr. Caldwell. He was excited about her interest.

"When you are ready for an internship, just give me a call. I will make a place for you."

How exciting the times were? Life was good, then she became pregnant. So many things changed. Suddenly life became very serious. She was carefree no more.

Nicole and Winston got married. Life was still good, just different. At eighteen she was a mother, and what a scary time that had been. Her mother, Charlene was her savior. Without her what would she have done? More importantly, what would Madison have done without her grand mom stepping up?

Nicole could honestly admit, she wasn't sure her baby girl would even be alive without her mom's help. How hard it was trying to go to school and be a mom and wife. How many tears were shed during that time? Finally, she gave up. She quit school and became a full-time mom.

Still, she eventually got her degrees in foreign languages and computer programing. Over the years she received a master's and a PhD in languages. She did volunteer work for the Memphis City School's language department, where she helped developed computer programs specializing in languages for the classrooms.

It was fun and rewarding, but that was a far as it went. All her special classes the schools had set up for her were for naught, for she never took advantage of the special gift God had given her.

In Memphis, most of their friends and associates were educated whites. There were plenty of different cultures in Memphis, she was just never around them much, so she rarely used her gift. She didn't really think about it, until she moved to New York.

Just walking down the streets of Manhattan, had awaken her gifts. Part of her wanted to pursue the idea of working at the United Nations. Yet, she had done nothing about that since her move. She had been procrastinating; had been wallowing in her sea of self-pity, then last night happened.

So, before she could even think about it, she picked up her phone and dialed the UN number their friend Jake had given her. As she listened to the dial tone, her heart raced. What was she doing? This was stupid, but just before she hung up a voice greeted her.

"Yes, I would like to speak with Mrs. Constance Norman please."

Back in Memphis, their longtime friend, who just happened to be a United State Senator, suggested she call Mrs. Norman. She remembered when Senator Jackson Freeman, "Jake" reached for Nicole's hand and drew her near.

"Nic, if you are still interested in talking with someone from the United Nations, I will let my friend Constance know to expect your call."

He smiled at her and continued.

"I want to help in any way I can. Just let me know when you are ready, and I will make it happen."

He hugged her, and that was that. All she had to do was let Jake know… that's all. So, earlier in the morning she texted him about thinking about making the call. And just like that she had an appointment the following Monday 1 pm.

Mrs. Norman told her to have the front desk notify her when she arrived.

"I will give you a tour and we can talk. Great, I will see you next Monday 1 pm. I am looking forward to meeting you. Senator Freeman is such a champion of yours."

God why had she done that. She just wanted to crawl back under the covers and hibernate in her tiny apartment. This was stupid, she didn't want to work at the U. N. or anywhere else for that matter. She had plenty of money. Winston saw to that. She didn't need to work. She would call them later and cancel. She didn't want a new life; she wanted her old one back.

In her mind she would cancel the appointment, however, she spent the next hours preparing for the meeting. It was in the early evening when she finished. She felt good, yet sad at the same time. Her days were filled with such sadness, her nights with despair.

"After last night, I can't keep living like this. I've got to start somewhere."

Maybe this was the answer. Jake's endorsement will make it much easier to get the job. Nicole had to laugh at the thought of a job. She hadn't had a real career job ever. Winston made tons of money and didn't want her to work.

Back when their daughter left for college, she mentioned to Winston about her thoughts of getting a job. A smile crossed her face as she remembered what he said.

"Babe, you have enough jobs already, what with all your charities, Madison, and most importantly, me. What else do you want?"

He gave her a long sexual kiss and patted her backside, and that was that.

"Damn you, why did you have to go and die on me? I know it has been over a year, and I should be doing better, but I am not, and then last night happened. Oh God, Winn, what am I going to do? You have always had all the answers, so now just tell me how in the world am I supposed to fix this, fix me?"

Nic grabbed a paper towel to blow her nose and dried her tears. She wadded the towel and threw it on the floor.

"And another thing, how am I supposed to get that look out of our daughter's eyes? You caused it you know. Now tell me how to erase it?"

Quietly she rose from her chair, picked up the wadded towel and put in the garbage, then she slowly moved down the hall to her bedroom. She crawled into bed.

"No, I caused all of this. I am the one. You shouldn't have been at that liquor store, all for the want of some stupid Chardonnay. I am so sorry, my love. You are gone because of me."
Soon she was fast asleep.

"Mother, why aren't you answering your phone? If you don't answer this text, I am coming over there. You are scaring me."
Nicole quickly texted back.

"Hi sweetie, I am sorry I didn't hear the phone, so sorry to worry you. Yes, I am fine, just taking a nap. My phone must have fallen under the pillow. Didn't hear it, so sorry."
Finally, she placated her daughter.

"You guys have a wonderful evening with your friends. Yes, I have plenty to eat. Love you, night, night."

Nicole put the phone down, rolled over and was back asleep with seconds. The morning light slipped through her bedroom window.

"God, another day…shit."

For three days and nights Nicole didn't leave her apartment. Her head hammered, and her stomach rumbled. She spent most of her time afraid to get out of bed, afraid to drink… afraid to think about what she had almost done.

Finally, it was Monday. Today was her appointment with Mrs. Norman at the U. N. Dragging herself out of bed took effort. With no energy, no care, she got herself dressed. Nicole glanced at the mirror as she put on her coat. She couldn't see how beautiful she was, how fabulous she looked in her black Armani suit and her white silk blouse. She pulled on her boots then placed a pair of black heels in her purse and headed out the door.

Moments later, she was on the streets in front of her building. She hadn't gotten used to Uber, so she went old school, raising her arm to hail a cab.

Twenty minutes later she was standing in front of the United Nations building. She paid the driver and began walking toward the entrance. Quickly she turned back toward the yellow cab, only to see it rushing out into traffic. Nicole sighed and started up the steps as if she was going to the guillotines.

Once inside, she headed toward the ladies' room to change her shoes, then went to the front desk.

"My name is Nicole Roberts. I have an appointment with Mrs. Constance Norman."

She took a seat and watched the world go by. So many different nationalities, so many different codes of dress. For a moment Nicole lost herself in the magnificence of all things United Nations.

"Mrs. Roberts, I'm Danielle Perry, Mrs. Norman's assistant."

Nicole was dumbstruck to see the model-like, stunningly beautiful dark-skinned young woman, with the most incredible eyes standing before her. Perhaps the most beautiful person she had ever laid eyes on. Nicole stood up and greeted her.

It took a moment for Nicole to close her mouth. She smiled and accepted Danielle's hand. Danielle didn't miss a beat. Obviously, she was used to people staring at her beauty.

"Senator Freeman mentioned you had just recently moved to New York. I hope your acclimation to our city is going well. Mrs. Norman will be with you shortly. Can I get you something to drink?"

"Water would be nice, thank you."

Nicole settled into one of the wingback chairs and took a deep breath.

"Mrs. Roberts, I am Constance Norman, I have heard so much about you from Senator Freeman."

She stood up and extended her hand.

"It is nice to meet you."

After two hours of conservation and a tour, Nicole said goodbye to Mrs. Norman and left the building.

Before she realized it, she had made her way up to second and fifty-sixth. Nicole noticed P. J. Clarks on the next block. She walked in, went to the back area and found a place to sit. She ordered a Diet Pepsi and one of their famous cheeseburgers.

She and Winn had been to PJ's many times over the years. He always marveled at the old bar nestled among the giant glass skyscrapers. In 1967, the restaurant owners refused to sell to developers. The New York Times described it as a "David vs Goliath" story, with David winning. And today, it works well for both. PJ's had always been a special place for Winn and Nicole but now all she felt was dark emptiness.

Was it ever going to get better, or was she just going to be unbearably sad for the rest of her life? Her thoughts went to what she had almost done to herself. Quickly, she blocked it out. She just couldn't handle thinking about that right now.

After a few minutes, Nicole pushed aside her barely touched burger, left three times more cash than necessary, and walked out.

The following week, when the snow had melted, she talked her daughter into letting her take Tank out to the park. Walking the little Yorkie was the one thing she could count on that didn't make her sad. She and Tank headed for the doggie park. What would New Yorkers do without these designated parks for the canine population?

As she tossed the tennis ball for Tank to fetch, Nicole watched the other dog owners interact with their pets. One thing for sure, New York loved their dogs.

Nicole made another ball toss and watched as Tank raced toward it. She found herself standing fairly close to a young couple who were in the doggie park with their little Yorkie. She turned and smiled, as she overheard them speaking Spanish. She understood the words they spoke.

All her life, she could translate the spoken words of most languages. It was her God given gift and now that she was living in New York, the sea of words spoken on the streets, awakened her language recognition skills that she had let lay dormant for so many years. She found it easy to decipher almost any language she overheard. She was beginning to like walking around Manhattan just listening. More and more each week she would walk and listen. It had become therapeutic to her. It kept the dark at bay. Today, she listened to the Spanish couple talking about how excited they were to be going out of town for the weekend.

He began describing all the things he was going to do to pleasure her. The young lady giggled, and Nicole eased around the tree to give them privacy.

Another toss, and Tank was off to chase the green ball. Once again, Nicole found herself listening to another conversation. It was just so easy for her. This time it was two Russian men speaking. They were discussing where and when the next drop would take place. She was sure she recognized the words; young girls.

As hard as she tried not to look their way, she couldn't help it. For just a fraction of a second, she glanced in their direction as a pair of cold hard eyes seem to zero in on her.

Shear panic flooded her veins. She almost stumbled over one of the dogs. Nicole quickly scooped up Tank and began making her way out of the doggie park. A black unmarked van swerved to keep from hitting her as she raced into the street. The driver cursed at her in Russian.

"Please God, don't let them follow me."
Nicole made a quick dash into the nearest Duane Reade store. Her heart pounded.

"Tankie, stop wiggling, please be still."

Finally, Nicole gathered enough courage to go outside. No one was waiting. Still, she practically ran to the Fetch Club and dropped Tank off, then raced to her home.

Chapter 2

As Nicole entered the safety of her apartment, a young man across from Manhattan, in a town called Kearny, New Jersey had no safe place. He was bound, held against his will in a dark, dingy basement below student housing. One of the men charged with watching over the young students was doing unspeakable things to this boy. No matter how much the boy begged and pleaded for him to stop. It only made the man do more.

As far as everyone knew, Mr. Adams was a pillar of the community. He was always kind and helpful to the boys. Almost no one knew his darkness. When the school year began, Adams would quietly search for his prey among the new students. He was generous with his time and all the students, so when he was nice to a certain boy, nothing stood out. Choosing the one and luring him into his secret room in the basement was almost as exciting as the actual act.

This year, the boy's name was Pavel. The first time Mr. Adams asked the young Russian student to help him carry some boxes to the storage room in the basement, he was happy to help. Little did Pavel know what was about to happen to him. It had been over two months since the nightmare began. No matter what, he still had to attend classes and do the work assigned to him, yet he lived under dark dread every minute. He knew when Mr. Adams beckoned him, he had no choice but to obey. He had to go and let him do horrible things to him. He saw no way out. Today, he laid tied up, while Adams gave several swipes on his backside with his riding crop to enhance his pleasure. Adams loved it when Pavel twisted and turned, pleading for him to stop. Finally, when he finished, he untied him, threw a couple of twenty-dollar bills on his young body. He reminded him what would happen to him and his family back home, if he told anyone.

"I own you boy, now go clean yourself up and get to class. You don't want to be late. I will be watching you."

Adams gave him another swipe and ordered him to go.

"HOLY CRAP SHIT, I am officially crazy."

Nicole double checked her locks door before making a beeline to the kitchen. Her hands shook hard as she poured a glass of wine, her first glass in a while. She needed it, she justified.

"I am certifiable, there is no other explanation. It has been a while since I have concentrated on any of the Russian dialects. I probably misunderstood what those men were saying."

Still she kept rolling it over and over in her head. Nicole was well into her second glass when her cell phone rang.

"Oh, hi Jake, it is good to hear your voice."

She lied.

"I am in the city for a few days, so I thought I would give you a call. Wanted to see how the interview went."

After a few more minutes of small talk Jake suggested they have dinner together. The last thing she wanted to do was go out to eat with Jake or anyone else, still, being raised to be a southern lady, made her suggest that he come over to her apartment for dinner.

"I can order Adrianne's pizza and salad if you would like. One of the great things about living here is vertically everything can be delivered to your door."

"Okay, great. See you around seven."

Immediately, she began tidying up her apartment.

"Damnit, why couldn't I have just said no? Why do we southern women act like this? Why can't we say no, I just want to be alone?"

Jake had been their friend for many years. He and Winston were in the same class at the University of Tennessee. They both played on the Vols football team.

They were each other's best man in their weddings. They spent so much time together, even after Jake's divorce years ago.

Nicole had never liked Jake's wife Mary all that much. It was always a struggle to be around such a negative, person. So, when she left him, Nicole was relieved. She had heard Mary had married some mega wealthy person and was living the good life overseas.

Jake never remarried. Shortly after their divorce, he became involved in politics. He was now half-way through his third term as one of Tennessee's United States Senators.

By the time 7 pm rolled around, she was in full dread mode. Why had she said yes?

Jake arrived armed with a bottle of very expensive Merlot, and a box of Memphis Dinstuhl's Chocolates. Even though they had greeted each other with hugs over the past years, this time it felt weird when he drew her in his arms.

"It is so good to see you Nicole."

A few moments later the doorbell rang announcing the pizza delivery. He handed her the bottle of wine.

"How about I take care of the Pizza, while you pour us a glass?"

She hadn't realized until much later in the evening that she was actually enjoying herself. Food was good, conversation was easy and fun, just like old time, except… darkness began to consume her body, guilt blanketed her soul.

Jake sat down his wine glass and leaned in.

"I wondered how long it would take for one of us to feel it."

Nicole looked up him, confused.

He continued.

"How long to feel the loss, the guilt. Sometimes it is overwhelming for me. I can only imagine what it is for you."
Jake retrieved his glass and turned to Nicole.

"I almost called you back to cancel but didn't. I just wanted to see you, to check on you. To be with…"
Jake stopped what he was about to say and moved closer to Nicole.

"You know, we both loved Winn. God, he was like my brother, hell, he was my brother. And I know how much you guys loved each other. But tonight, I just needed to be with my good friend. Like old times."
The words "like old times" were like a key unlocking a wave of pain stabbing through her. She tried to catch her breath. She beat at her chest trying to open her air waves. Suddenly a flood of tears began streaming down her face. She couldn't help herself. She couldn't stop.

Silently, he wrapped his arms around her as they snuggled together on the couch. Eventually, they both dozed off.
It was a few minutes past ten when her daughter texted her mom a good night message. Thankfully, Nicole woke up when she felt her iPhone buzz. Quickly, she texted her usual message back, then slowly eased herself out of Jake's arms. They had fallen asleep sitting up. She scooted to the other end of the couch and watched him as he slept.

She had never thought much about Jake as a man. It was always Jake and Mary as a couple, or Jake as Winn's best friend, as her friend. But tonight, she looked at him, saw how handsome he was. He was in excellent shape, and his unusually colored eyes set him apart. Most importantly he was a good and kind man.

Nicole smiled slightly as she remembered Winn teasing Jake about what a nice guy like him was doing in the Senate. Even though he was on his third term, he never seems to let the atmosphere of greed and corruption jade him. He had accomplished good things for Tennessee.

She reached for the throw and covered his legs, being careful not to wake him. She scooted off the couch, picked up the glasses and deposited them in the kitchen sink. She would wash them tomorrow. She walked to her bedroom and closed the door.

As she lay in bed, she continued her thoughts of Jake. She wondered why he had never remarried. She also wondered if he had a girlfriend. She had seen his pictures in the People magazine, page six and such, escorting many beautiful women over the years, but no one seem to stick. She wondered why. Finally, she turned off her light.

For once, Nicole slept through the night. Maybe she was turning a corner. She smiled and stretched lazily remembering last night. Suddenly it hit her. There was a man in her apartment.

Grabbing clothes from her closet, she raced to the bathroom, showered quickly, brushed hair and teeth, threw clothes on and went into the living room.

To her relief and dismay, Jake was not there. The couch had been straightened, and the wine glasses washed.

It was if last night didn't happen. Well, not that anything happened, it was as if he had never been there. Nicole reached in the frig. for a diet Pepsi then walked back to the living room looking for a note.

"Where are your manners my friend, the courteous thing would have been to leave a note."

Just then, the outside buzzer rang, causing Nicole to jump. Jake's deep voice sounded over the intercom.

"I have hot bagels and juice."

Nicole couldn't help but laugh as she buzzed him in. A man in her apartment was all too weird.

He made his way into her kitchen, dumping the packages on the counter.

"I hope you like bagels."

He turned and smiled sheepishly.

"Well, damn, I can't believe I fell asleep on your couch. I must have had more wine than I realized."

He smiled again and shook his head.

"But Nic, I actually slept the whole night. Don't know how long it has been since I've done that."

Nic fumbled with the glass of juice.

"Would you like to freshen up, shower? There are extra toothbrushes, towels and stuff in the cabinet."

She pointed down the hall to the guest bathroom.

"Yes, if you don't mind, I will take you up on your offer. I have an early meeting, and this will save time."

He turned toward the bathroom.

A few minutes later her daughter called.

"Good morning sweet angel."

"Morning mom. What are you up to this morning?" Nicole could feel her face heat up. Guilt flooded her veins.

"Oh nothing. Just getting the day started. How about you? Are you on your way to work?"

"Yes, got a big event coming up tomorrow night, so I have tons to do. I was just thinking maybe you would like to come to this one. It should be fun. We are launching Mimeo's new designs, and I have a list of cool celebs attending. Everyone loves her designs. Zack is coming, do you want to go with him?"

At that moment, Jake walked into the kitchen.

"Every time I come to New York, I have to get R and B bagels. They are the best... oops... sorry... didn't realize you were on the phone."

"Mom, is someone there? Are you all right?"

Once again Nicole's face turned beet red. Heat exploded through her body. Her voice was a couple of octaves higher.

"Yes, you will never believe who came into town, Uncle Jake. He just stopped by this morning, early to check on me, wasn't that nice. He brought hot bagels. He is in town for meetings, so he came by early before his meetings on Senate business, you know, in town on Senate business... yes. He just came by, early, and brought bagels, they are hot...."

God, she had to shut up. She covered her mouth to keep from saying anything else. She turned to Jake. He had a big grin on his face as he reached for the phone and began talking as if it were nothing.

"How's my favorite godchild? By the way, congrats on your promotion, your mom told me about it. You are amazing." He took a sip of his coffee and continued.

"I just stopped by to check on your mom. I know it's early, but she was kind enough to let me come by anyway."

Nic watched in amazement as Jake talked to her daughter. Of course, they had known each other since Madison was born. She and Winston had asked Jake to be Madison's god parent. It is an Episcopal tradition.

"Yes, I am in town for the rest of the week. Yes, that sounds like fun. I would love to come to your event tomorrow night. I have been wanting to see you work your magic. If there is anything I can do to help, just let me know? Well, yes, of course you can put me on your press release list. I would be honored. Yes, you too, here is your mom."

"Mom, I have to go, got a meeting. I am excited that Uncle Jake is coming to my event. Oh, and if you want to walk Tank today, he is at the Fetch club. Love you, gotta run."

"Love you."

Jake laughed.

"Why do I feel as if we've just been caught red handed behind the barn so to speak?"

They both laughed hard, they were having fun. Then that same awkwardness and guilt began to creep in.

"Look, I have to go, I really do have a meeting this morning. I am talking with the Police Commissioner about New York's "See Something, Say Something" program. I'm going to meet with the Commissioner and see firsthand how it works and what it would take to set up a program like that for Tennessee."

Jake finished his bagel.

"In today's world, all of our states should have this kind of program. The people need to be more aware of what to do. Who to contact if something happens? The school shootings are the big reason to do something. Our kids are just too vulnerable. They especially need to know what to do."

He looked at Nicole for a moment.

"What is it, is something wrong? Are you okay?"

"No, no everything is fine."

She finished taking a sip of her diet drink and set it down.

"Well, not actually… I'm not sure. It was probably nothing, just my imagination."

He put his hand on her shoulders then quickly removed it.

"Tell me."

"You know how I am about knowing different languages. Remember the language games the three of us used to play back at UT. Well, yesterday, while I was at the dog park with Tank, I overheard some guys talking. It was a Siberian Turkic dialect. They said something about young girls. I could have been wrong, I probably misunderstood, but to be honest it was disturbing. Jake, if I am right, they were talking about trafficking young girls."

Nicole placed her hands over her mouth.

"Oh my god, what kind of person am I? You called and came over… and … I forgot all about what those men said. I am a horrible person. I forgot."

She took a deep breath and began again.

"I don't know for sure if I overheard them correctly. I could have been wrong. I really don't know what to do."

"I have never known anyone who could interpret languages like you do, so I say you heard correctly. Look, this is exactly what

I'm talking about. People need to be aware of what to do, who to call."

Jake began to put his overcoat on as he continued.

"Do you remember anything else? Did they say a time or location?"

"No, I don't think so, I can't remember."

"Just let me know if you remember anything else. I will pass this along to the right people."

Jake glanced at this watch.

"Gotta run."

He reached the door, then turned to her.

"Nic, thanks for last night. Enjoyed myself. And thanks for letting me sleep on your couch."

He stopped for a moment and just looked at her, then signed.

"I'll call you when I am done."

He opened the door and was gone, leaving an unsettled feeling in her, not a bad feeling, just unsettling.

After riding her stationary bike for an hour, she took a long shower. As she reached to turn the water off, the phone rang. She quickly wrapped a towel around her body and picked up her cell. Caller ID showed it was Jake.

"Hi Nicole, hope I didn't disturb, but I am in my meeting with the Police Commissioner. I took the liberty of mentioning what you told me this morning about the conversation you overheard. The Commissioner wants to know if you remember anything else."

"Well, actually, I think I overheard one of them saying something about meeting at Mandies. I am not exactly sure about that, but it was something close to it. And there was a big black unmarked van that nearly ran over me. Not sure if that had anything to do with anything, but they yelled at me in the same Turkic dialect. Don't know why I am remembering that. Sorry I didn't get the plate number. Not sure if any of that is helpful."

"It is all helpful. I will call you back shortly. Thanks Nicole."

Jake hung up and continued talking with the Commissioner. He had a proposal to run by him that would be beneficial to them both.

After she dried her hair and finished dressing, she sat down on the couch. She took a deep breath and smiled. The dark heaviness that had been surrounding her for over a year, was not quite so heavy this morning. Maybe she was finally getting better.

"Winston, I love you so much, my heart aches all the time. Why did you leave me? I am so sorry."

She wiped the tears from her face, just as the phone rang. It was Jake again.

"At last, I am through with my meeting. Wait, is something wrong? Are you okay?"

"No everything is fine, just having a moment."

"Oh, I see."

But he didn't.

"Hope you didn't mind me mentioning our conversation to the Commissioner. He said to tell you thanks. Listen, I was wondering if I could pick you up tomorrow night to go to Madison's event."

"I would appreciate it. I don't want to go alone; you have no idea."

He laughed but didn't finish his thoughts.

"My car could pick up Zack as well if he wants."

"Let me get back with you."

A few minutes later the phone rang again. Gees, so many calls. I usually get a text a day from my daughter, that is all. She laughed at herself, now I am Miss popular.

This time the call was from the UN.

"Hello, Mrs. Roberts. This is Danielle Perry from Mrs. Norman's office. We are emailing forms to you concerning your employment with the UN. Just fill them out and return as soon as possible. We are looking forward to working with you. Have a pleasant day?"

Nic said goodbye and chastised herself because she had not even given her interview another thought. However, instead of waiting for the email, she turned and headed to the kitchen. Her cell rang again.

"Gee, enough already."

When she saw it was Madison, she happily picked up the phone.

"Hi baby."

"Hi mom, I only have a minute, wanted you to know you are officially on the invite list. Just talked to Uncle Jake, and guess what? He said the Police Commissioner wants to come to the event. Uncle Jake is awesome! This is turning out to be a really big deal. Got to run, oh, Uncle Jake said he would pick you up, so be ready by 6 pm. Wear something nice, dressy causal, and if you need me to go online and find you something just let me know."

Before she could answer, Madison had already hung up.

Suddenly, there was so much going on. Things to plan. Maybe being busy would be a good thing. Maybe it would keep the darkness at bay.

The next morning, Nicole busied herself searching her closet for something to wear to Madison's event. Finally, she settled on a long sleeve black silk dress. She liked the way it felt and flowed on her body. The last time she wore it was about a month before Winn had been killed. They had gone to a fundraiser for St. Jude in Memphis. Nicole eased back on her bed, closed her eyes and remembered. This was one of those near perfect nights. What fun they had being with friends that night? She bowed her head thinking if only she had known. A tear dropped from her eye.

Quickly, she stood up as she tried to shake the darkness that followed such memories. She made herself select accessories. Once satisfied, she picked up the TV remote, punched the on button to the news station. She walked over to her stationary bike and began her ride.

About ten minutes into her ride, she glanced at the TV screen. Someone had jumped from a building. They were showing a picture of a student from the University housed in the building where her attorney was located. The University's name and address ran across the bottom of the screen.

As the news anchor showed a picture of the young man that had jumped but withheld his name. Nic turned the sound up and leaned in to get a better look at the boy's photo. He looked similar to one of the boys on the elevator, however, she hadn't looked at them that closely, so she couldn't be sure. The students hung around the lobby, but she never took the time to engage. It was all so sad.

Kids were lucky to get the opportunity to go to a college, however, people forget or didn't realize just how stressful higher education can be. Everything is so intense. She wondered if anyone had ever done a study on just how many kids have tried and how many succeeded in taking their lives while pursing higher education. She made a mental note to google that later.

The weight of what she had almost done was still heavy on her mind.

Chapter 3

In the conference room at the University, three men were meeting to discuss the effects of the young man that jumped.

"Fortunately, I have people at Police Headquarters, and the examiner's office. The boy's death has been ruled a suicide. There will be no mention of what had been done to the kid, no further investigation. However, we have a light on us now. I can't allow this kind of shenanigans. We have built a very successful organization; however, I will not hesitate to shut everything down, I mean everything."

He paused to take a sip of his drink while he made sure the two men understood exactly what he meant.

"Adams must be dealt with. Why didn't anyone realize he was screwing that kid? The examiner said the boy had been beaten and raped repeatedly over a period of months. He must have jumped as a last resort. Get Pence on this. I don't want Adams permanently gone yet. Right now, it would not be smart. Send Pence and his men to talk to him. He will know what to do. If Adams doesn't straighten up by school's end, I want his ass wiped off this earth."

He finished the rest of his drank and rose from the table.

"Gentlemen, I have an event to attend."

He left, while the two other men continued the meeting.

The evening came around quickly. Nicole was dressed by five-forty. She poured herself a glass of champagne and tuned on Pandora music. Nic flipped channels on the muted TV looking for more information about the student that took his life. She didn't find anything new.

She walked over to the mirror to recheck her make-up. How different this evening would be? So many times, before she had attended events with Winston. Many times, Jake had joined them. Yes, tonight would be different, sad and weird, yet part of her was looking forward to getting out like this again.

"Oh Winn, why can't you be here tonight with our beautiful daughter. You would be so proud of her."

The door buzzed at exactly six pm. As she opened the door, Jake just stood frozen and stared at her.

"My God, you are beautiful."

Nicole laughed and returned the compliment.

"You look quite handsome in that... Is it an Armani?"

He looked in wonder down at his suit.

"Yes, actually it is."

She thought she noticed a slight redness in Jake's cheeks. Another something different to go along with this very different evening. He helped with her coat and they were on their way.

"By the way, Madison is so happy that you talked the Commissioner into coming to her event. She is beyond excited. Not that she will show it of course."

"Actually, it was easy, he wanted to come."

The town car stopped in front of the beautiful arched glass Winter Palace. Minutes later, they were on their way up the steps and into the evening. The words Mama Proud couldn't come close to describing how Nicole felt about her daughter. Her beautiful Madison was the star of the night.

Jake took two champagne glasses from the waiter and offered Nicole one. He placed his hand on her elbow turning her toward him, when a highly tailored, impeccably dressed, silver haired man walked up next to Jake. She thought she had seen him somewhere, but she couldn't place him.

"Hello Jake, heard you were in our fair city."
He offered his hand to shake. Nicole sensed reluctance in Jake.

"Donald."
The man smiled and turned toward Nicole.

"Jake, how do you manage to find the most beautiful creatures to accompany you to these tedious affairs. Hello, I am Donald Billings."
At that moment a beautiful dressed young lady joined them. She stood beside Mr. Billings and smiled.

"Let me introduce my ward, Carrie James, she is here on scholarship."

Carrie smiled and offered her hand.

"A pleasure to meet you."

Mr. Billings immediately took over the conservation.

"Nicole, are you from New York?"

"Donald, my apologies, but we are being summoned, please excuse us. It was a pleasure meeting you Miss James."

He took Nicole arm as they walked away.

"Sorry about that, but he was gearing up to find out as much as he could about you. Besides being a blowhard, he is a gossip whore."

She laughed.

"Well, within ten-seconds, he called me a creature, and my daughter's event a tedious affair, so, no, I am not a fan."

As they made their way over to the Commissioner, Nicole looked back at Carrie James.

"She is stunningly beautiful".

Jake intervened.

"The real question is, what is she doing with the likes of Billings?"

Nicole's mind lingered on Donald Billings for a moment. He looked vaguely familiar, then decided she must have seen his photo in the newspaper or somewhere.

"Commissioner, this is Nicole Roberts."

The larger than life, very handsome, very tall, charismatic gentleman covered her extended hand with his own. Nic had seen him on TV many times in the news. Always thought he was handsome, but she had no idea just how good looking he really was. She made herself stop staring.

"Nice to meet you Mrs. Roberts. Jake has been singing your praises all day. And I must say your daughter knows how to put on an event, great gathering."

"Thank you for taking the time out of your busy schedule to lend your support."

"Nonsense, I am really enjoying myself, besides I asked the Senator if I could join him tonight. You see, I have an ulterior motive."

He turned and looked directly at her. She could feel the pull of his intensity.

"You are the reason I am here."

Nicole was completely confused.

"Pardon."

"I was fascinated by what Jake told me concerning your extraordinary language abilities. It is a very rare gift, Mrs. Roberts, very rare indeed."

"Thank you, and please call me Nicole."

"Okay, and I am Frank."

At that moment three beautiful young ladies came up to Jake and began a conversation. The Commissioner steered her around to a more private area. His bodyguard keeping close tabs yet standing off to the side. Frank looked at him, and suddenly two glasses of champagne appeared. He took them, handing her one.

"Your unique gift is of interest to me. Jake tells me it is something you have been able to do since you were quite young." The Commissioner sat his glass down on a nearby table and continued.

"Would it be convenient for you to join our breakfast meeting tomorrow morning ten am, in my office? We are forming a task force to find new ways to keep our city safe. Hearing your story gave me an idea. I can have a car for you say tomorrow, 9:10 am."

"I am flattered Mr. I mean Frank, but I am just a house... was just a housewife. I am surely not qualified for such an endeavor."

"Let me be the judge of that, Nicole. Do not think I would waste yours, or my time, or more importantly, the taxpayer's money if I didn't think you could be of help. And do not think I wouldn't have already vetted you, so I know you are very well qualified." He picked up his glass and drank the rest of his champagne.

"This is a serious offer on a very serious matter." He paused and looked at her intently, waiting for her answer.

She took a sip of her champagne then answered.

"Well, if you think I could be of help, I would be honored to join you tomorrow morning."

"Great, a car will be at your home, 9:10 am."

"My address is…"

He put his hand up to stop her.

"No need."

The Commissioner smiled at her, then turned to his bodyguard and suddenly they were off. Nicole smiled as she watched them leave the building. As if on cue, Jake moved to her side.

"Well, what do you think about the Commissioner?"

"Wow!"

They both laughed.

As they walked toward Madison, Nicole told Jake about the Commissioner's request.

"Did you know he was going to do this?"

"I figured he was but didn't know for sure. I will be at the breakfast meeting as well. He asked me to sit in, probably in part because of you, plus partly because I am on the Senate Homeland Security Committee."

"Well, not because of me, he didn't know I would say yes."

Jake laughed.

"Say no to that man? Who are you kidding?"

They laughed again.

"Sweetie, what an amazing event, I am so proud of you."

"Thanks mom and thanks Uncle Jake. When folks heard you as well as the Commissioner were going to be here, there were several last-minute requests from high profile people to join the event. The execs are beyond pleased."

Nicole and Jake said their goodbyes and began making their way toward the door. Nic felt eyes on her. She turned and saw Mr. Billings looking at her and Jake. Chills shot up her spine. Something about that man. She couldn't place it but there was something. She was relieved when they finally got into the limousine and headed home.

Jake went with her up the elevator to her apartment. She smiled and waited while he took her key to unlock her door.

"I really enjoyed the evening. You and my goddaughter are amazing."

He gave her back her keys.

"Shall I pick you up in the morning?"

"No, he is sending a car."

"Well, see you in the morning."

He gave her a quick hug and walked to the elevator. After hanging up her clothes, she stepped into the shower. Her head was spinning. Things were happening too fast. She dried off and put on her nightgown, then crawled into bed.

"I don't want to go tomorrow. Why did I say yes? Winn, things are happening too fast. I just want to stay in my apartment, in my bed. Make this all go away."

Tears fell until she slept.

Dark dreams filled her night. Black vans filled with blood poured from their doors. Young girls were being tossed out the windows. Bare tree limbs bending from the strong winds whirling around her. She was drenched, her heart pounding. She glanced at her clock. It was 4:30 am. Her nightmares were always dark, but this one was more horrible than most. The talk of the young girls must have brought this one on.

"Damn, I thought I was getting better."

She got out of bed and went to the kitchen.

"Water, drink water, stupid."

Her hand shook. She crawled back in bed, then double checked her alarm clock.

9:10 am on the dot, the car picked her up. Her heart was racing as the car drove to the Police headquarters. The driver escorted her up the steps where she was met by a well-dressed gentleman.

"Good morning Mrs. Roberts, I am Gary Goodhouse, the Commissioner's assistant."

He had already started down the hall, so she followed. When they entered, the Commissioner rose from his chair at the head of the Conference table.

"Nicole, good to see you. Please have a seat."

He pulled out the chair to his right and she sat. She made a quick search for Jake. He was at the other end of the table. He gave her a smile. Introductions were quickly made and then down to business. Ninety minutes later, the meeting was over. Her head was spinning from trying to keep up.

Everything was in rapid fire mode. So many brilliant minds sharing their thoughts, and ideas on how to make their city a safer place. Jake contributed heavily to the discussions, especially when it concerned government interactions. Everyone seemed to hang on his every word.

She just listened. Didn't have the nerve to interact. She wasn't for sure she had any thoughts. It was all too fast. Her heart raced. She tried not to show it, but she was having trouble breathing. As they walked into the hall, she could feel her body going into panic mode. She had to get out of there. Jake came up behind her and asked if she wanted to get something to eat. She nodded yes, anything to get out of there. As they turned to leave, the Commissioner walked up.

"Before you go, Nicole, would you check with Gary for a convenient time to meet with the group."

He shook hands with them both and was off. His bodyguard right behind him.

"Would tomorrow 3 pm work for you? We can meet in the conference room."

He already had the time marked in his table before she could nod affirmative.

"Good, do you need a car?"

"No, thank you."

She didn't want to impose.

Jake placed his hand on her back as they started toward the door.

"You know anytime the city offers a car, you should take it. They have tons of them, and it is much easier getting around the city."

With a shaky voice she implored.

"Can we go?"

After they were seated at the Grey Goose restaurant in the West Village, she finally could steady her breath.

"What was that all about? Why on earth was I invited and why am I going back tomorrow?"

"I guess you will find out tomorrow, but I would think it has to do with your language recognition skills."

Nicole leaned in.

"Jake, I have never done anything with my 'language recognition skills."

She raised her hands to make quotation signs.

"Nonsense, you have done a lot for the Memphis public schools, so stop selling yourself short."

Jake reached for her hand across the table. Heat flooded her body. Why was he touching her that way? This is Jake for Christ Sake. She pulled her hand back quickly and opened the menu.

"Shall we order?"

3 pm came shockingly fast the next day. Nicole took a deep breath as she walked into the waiting area. She couldn't peel out of her heavy coat fast enough. Even though it was twenty-nine degrees outside, she was sweating. Her head was spinning, her hands shaking.

"Gee's Nic, stop being so stupid."

A quick glance at her watch told her she had just enough time to freshen up. She turned toward the ladies' room, only to slam into a man in a grey suit.

"Oh, I'm terribly sorry."

"You need to watch where you are going."

That was unsettling to say the least. She made her way to the ladies' room. She wanted to stay in there but knew she couldn't. The moment she returned to the reception area, Mr. Goodhouse was standing, waiting.

"I am sorry to keep…"

"This way please, everyone is waiting."

She softly said.

"I'm sorry."

She could feel her face heating up. The conference room was filled with business suited young adults all taping away on their laptops. The clicking sound came to an abrupt halt the moment Mr. Goodhouse cleared his throat.

"Mr. Thomas will join you momentarily."

"Listen up everyone, this is Mrs. Nicole Roberts. The Commissioner wants her involved with this project, so play nice and let's get her up to speed."

A young woman in a navy suit walked up next to her.

"Hello, I'm Jenny. We usually aren't this rude, but we are under the gun on a major project. The deadline is just hours away." She motioned for Nicole to take a seat.

"Please."

Nicole sat silently watching the young group power through with lighting speed. She was amazed how fast they spoke to each other. They were schooled in this. They knew what they were doing, she did not. This was like a foreign language that she couldn't understand. She chuckled aloud at that thought. Everyone turned to stare. She lowered her head and patted the sweat on her upper lips.

Less than seventy-two hours ago she could hardly get out of bed, hadn't wanted to for months, and now suddenly she's needed on a task force for one of the most powerful cities in the world.

The whole thing is just too crazy. She had to get out of there.

Nicole rose from her chair just as the conference room door opened. All eyes turned to her, then to the door. Nowhere to run nowhere to hide. She eased back into her seat.

"Mrs. Roberts, I am Jason Thomas. I will be taking point on this project, so if you have any questions don't hesitate to ask. Now, shall we begin?"

It was almost six pm when she emerged from the conference room. Everyone else left at five, but she was asked to stay. Mr. Thomas wanted to go over some things with her.

As she walked out into the cold windy night, she turned to see that unsmiling man in the grey suit she had bumped into earlier. He looked at her. She smiled, he did not. He turned and walked away.

"Jerk."

The car service police headquarters provided her came to a stop near where she was standing. Just as she settled into the back seat of the town car, her daughter called.

"Hi sweetie, yes, I am just leaving for home now. No, I took them up on their kind offer of a car. I could get used to this. No, sweetie, can I take a raincheck? I think I am going to just go straight home and get into bed. No, I haven't even thought about dinner. Oh yes, that would be great. I should be home in about twenty minutes. You are awesome to order dinner for me. Now that I think about it, I am starving."

She twisted around in her seat.

"Yes, it was a good meeting. My head is overflowing with information. Maybe we could get together this weekend. Would love to get your prospective. Yes, tomorrow night sounds great. Besides, I miss being with my grand puppy. How is the cutie pie doing? Okay, sweetie, see you tomorrow night around seven. Love you bunches."

She thanked the driver, retrieved her purse and the new leather bag given to her by Mr. Thomas. Inside was a new apple laptop. Evidently, it was scribed, scrambled, and whatever else they said at the meeting.

Mr. Thomas got very serious when he gave it to her.

"This is to be used by you only for the business at hand only. Please know that anything you do on this laptop will be monitored, everything. We all have to be very careful, for the safety of everyone."

With that he handed her the case, however, he held onto it for a couple of seconds before he let go, as if to emphasize the importance of entrusting her with such a serious instrument.

Chapter 4

As soon as Nicole walked into her apartment, she locked the door, sat her purse and new leather case down, pulled off her coat, and placed everything in the entry closet. Next came her boots, then her bra. She smiled as she rubbed her chest.

"Nothing like the feel of freedom."

As if on cue, the front desk buzz to announce the delivery of food.

"Oops."

She had already forgotten her daughter's offer of food.

"Well, too bad, the girls are free and they're staying that way."

Once money for nourishment was exchanged, she relocked the door. The grilled chicken salad and fresh hot bread from Adrianne's smelled delicious. She grabbed a wine glass, filled it and took everything to the living room. As she munched on her salad, her thoughts ran back over the meeting.

The past few days were essentially one big ball of haze. Her mind bounced from one thing to another. How had she gone from fighting off deep depression, not being able to get out of bed, and almost doing the unthinkable, to being on a very important task force for the New York City Police Department?

People of importance were asked on this kind of task force, not her. It was ridiculous, stupid ridiculous. One thing for sure, she was not qualified for such a gigantic undertaking. And yet, here she was with a new important laptop to prove it. Why on earth was she chosen? And suddenly, it came to her. She put down her plate on the coffee table and grabbed the phone.

Quickly, she punched in Jake's number. Before he could say anything more than hello, she rapidly fired questions back at him.

"Why me? Why would they choose me to be on such an important committee? Lord knows I am not qualified. Do you know how embarrassing this is going to be when they ask me to leave?"

"Nic."

She cut him off.

"And you know they will. These people know what they are doing. They are schooled in this. And what are my qualification? Oh, let me see, oh yes, I am the poor widow of your best friend who was murdered, because I was too worthless to get off my ass to go buy wine. I am the reason my husband is dead."

Tears were streaming down her face. Between gasping of breath, she tried to speak.

"I hate…"

"I am coming over."

"No, don't, I don't want you to."

He had already hung up.

"Well, Mr. Bigshot, too bad. I am so not going to let you in."

She downed the rest of her glass of wine, grabbed her salad and placed it in the refrigerator. She leaned against the kitchen counter and poured another glass, as the doorbell rang.

"No, not gonna happen."

Yet, as she was saying the words, she punched the button to give him assess.

"Damn, I didn't mean to do that."

Still, she opened the door, waiting.

Jake quickly raced to her side as she grabbed at him holding on for dear life.

He picked her up and carried her through the door.

"Say it damnit, say it. It is all my fault Winn is dead. My fault."

Gently he placed her on the couch walked back to lock the door, then pour them both a glass of wine. As he handed her the goblet, he pulled up a chair to get closer to her.

"Oh, Jake, forgive me, I am so embarrassed. I shouldn't have called. This is pathetic. I am so stupid."

"Do you realize how many times you call yourself stupid? You, a member of Mensa."

She kind of smiled, as she took a small sip of her wine. She was feeling the effects of her earlier guzzling.

"First, of all, the man who shot Winn is to blame. That man... not you."

Jake placed the chair back to its original spot and set on the couch beside Nicole.

"My therapist says that feeling guilty for being alive is normal. We just have to figure out ways to deal."

Her eyes got big.

"Wait a minute. You see a therapist?"

"Yes, I went to her after I divorced."

"Oh, Jake I didn't realize you were hurt by…"

"No, I didn't go to her because I was hurt, I went to her because I was so angry at myself. I was angry because I had let something go on for so long that shouldn't have started in the first place. But that is for another time. Why I am telling you this is because I went back to my therapist after Winn died. Nic, I could feel the anger filling my insides again. She calls it survivors blame or guilt, I forgot which one. Anyway, the point being, it is something we have to work through. I still have unguarded moments when anger seeps in, but I have learned the tools to cope. However, my sweet friend…"

He put his arms around her, and she leaned into him.

"If you feel like talking then let's talk. We can work through this together."

Nicole pulled away from him and crossed her legs facing him.

"It's been over a year since this nightmare started, and I am stuck. People tell me time will make things easier, but I am here to tell you that is a lie. I think I did better the first few months than now. I am so mad at myself for not getting better. Well, that is not true, because you see, most of the time I just don't give a damn about anything."

Jake placed his hand on her leg.

"I am a few steps ahead of you, because you see, I was in that don't give a damn faze, then jumped into major anger at everyone and everything. All that and trying to be a Senator at the same time. That was when I decided I needed help again, well actually it was Amanda who said either I go get help or she was going to quit."

He reached for his wine again.

"This may sound crazy, but I was even mad at the police for doing their job so quickly."

Nicole unfolded her long legs and practically jumped off the couch. She started to pace in front of him.

"Oh my god, I did the exact same thing."

She turned to face Jake.

"Sargent Johnson was so nice and considerate to us, so helpful, when it first happened. Then two days later, when the gunman was shot and killed it was all over. They had found the man that shot Winston, and he was killed in a gunfight. It was over, but I was still reeling from Winston being killed. It was not fair to them, however, when he told us what happened, basically wrapping things up I could hardly breathe. When he finished, Madison and I said goodbye and left. Then I realized I had dropped one of my gloves, so while Madison fetched the car, I went back upstairs to retrieve why glove. As I turned the corner, I saw the Sargent and his men giving each other the high five. Congratulating each other on a job well done. Then I overheard the Sargent tell his men that Winston was in the wrong place at the wrong time and in the wrong kind of car. He told them the shooter was apparently after someone else that happened to drive a car similar to Winston's. Evidently, he thought the car belonged to a man that was stealing drugs from him. He pulled out his gun and shot into the car."

"She overheard him say that if he hadn't pulled into that liquor store parking lot, he would be alive and well today." She took a big gulp of air.

"They didn't know I was there, didn't know I overheard them. Jake, he was there because of me, because I asked him to pick up a particular wine. I barely made it to the elevator. Fortunately, Madison had already pulled the car out front, waiting for me. It was all I could do to hold it together until we got home. I went straight to bed. Thank goodness Zack and Jim were there for Madison, because I certainly wasn't. The police had moved on to the next crime, but I was stuck in this one, and I have never been able to get unstuck."

She sat back down on the couch next to him. Jake reached out and pulled her to him. He wrapped his arms around her, and she let him. It felt good, safe,

They stayed that way for a while.

"Thank you for not listening to me, for coming over anyway."

He reached up and gently pushed back a string of hair behind her ear.

"I will always be here for you and Madison; you know that don't you."

She snuggled closer as she nodded her head slightly.

Jake leaned in and kissed her forehead.

Once again, they were still.

Her voice was a little more than a whisper.

"I think maybe I have been acting a little bit crazed since you have been here."

Nicole cleared her throat and began again.

"Jake, ever since Winn died, I have been living with this blanket of black nothingness. I go from deep depression to so much anger I can hardly breathe. I just go through the motions for Madison. I pretend all the time. I drink too much at night, just to get maybe a little sleep. Almost every night I have horrifying nightmares, when morning comes, and it starts all over again."

She twisted away from him, so she could look him in the eye.

"It has been over a year and I am worse, not better. I am so tired of being like this."

Nicole grabbed his sleeve and pulled him closer.

"Yet, this week I am suddenly invited to work with the Police Commissioner of New York for Christ sakes. One day I can't get out of bed, and the very next day I am on an important task force. While I appreciate what you are doing for me, trying to fix me, like forcing the Police Commissioner to hire me, but you have thrown me into something I can't possible handle."

It was Jake's turn to pull away.

"First of all, let me be perfectly clear, I did not... let me repeat, did not force Frank into hiring you."

Jake knew what he was saying wasn't completely true, but she didn't need to know.

"All I did was tell him what you overheard at the park, and I did that to emphasize my agenda about taking the See Something, Say Something program to Tennessee."

Jake got up and sat in the chair opposite the couch.

He stopped when he noticed she was shaking.

"Are you okay?"

She rubbed her arms.

"Yes, I am fine."

He stared for a moment, then continued.

"Frank was the one who insisted on meeting you. He invited himself to Madison's event when I mentioned we were going. His new team got a big boost last night based on what happened with the Russian raid."

She just looked at him.

"Wait, didn't they tell you? I assumed that was what the meeting was about today."

"I don't know what you are talking about."

"Well, the tip you gave them panned out. Since 911, NSA has made so much progress in tracing internet chatter, that some of the terrorist groups are going old school. They are forming small cells that meet out in the open, in parks and such. It is so much harder to keep track. You, overhearing their plans like you did, gave the task force new avenues to pursue. When you remembered those men mentioning Mandie's Place that was all they needed. Evidently, they have been undercover for months trying to get these guys. It wasn't Mandie's but it was close enough for them to figure out where the meeting was being held. The special units got there just in time to save a truck filled with girls."

"Oh My God... are you serious?"

Jake noticed a quick spark in her eyes. One that had been gone for over a year.

"Jake that is wonderful. Thank goodness you were here to know what to do."

He smiled and sat back down beside her, this time he couldn't help himself. He put his arm around her.

"We make a pretty good team."

He leaned in and gently kissed her on her cheek.

Old Mr. Awkwardness raised its head again. Jake unfolded his arms and long legs then stood up.

"Well, guess I had better get going."

Before she realized it, Nicole burst out.

"NO!"

Quickly, she jumped up trying to cover up her outburst.

"Madison just sent over an enormous grilled chicken salad with the most amazing bread. Way more than I could possibly eat, please join me."

Jake stared for a moment, then smiled.

"Well, you only have to ask me once, for I am starving."

They laughed as the two made their way to the kitchen.

She poured them one more glass of wine.

"Look we can worry about our wine consumption another day, just not tonight."

While they ate, Jake told her about the meetings he had attended the last couple of days.

"I have had a couple of very exciting days. Nic, I have been listening to experts from around the world speak about global warming. There are so many amazing minds of this... so many things going on. Increased investments are finally coming together for research on how to lower the carbon footprint. We have got to find a way to get clean affordable energy to the greatest number of people on the planet. Several foundations like the Gates Foundation, Jack Ma of Alibaba Group, Philanthropist Tom Steyer, just to name a few are very much involved in finding a solution to probably this biggest problem of our time."

He took a large bite of the bread.

"I am on the climate change committee. Yes, we finally got the Senate to form a committee, and that took forever. So many of our supposedly intelligent leaders don't believe there is a problem, or shall we say their Super Pacs tell them there is no problem. It is crazy. Some Senators are fighting against the wind turbines being built in the mountains. They are so owned by the Pacs they won't even consider the damage they are doing. There is nothing right about any of this, however, these Senators keep getting elected. That is where I fault the citizens. They need to educate themselves about what is going on, and then vote. Okay, I am stepping off my soap box now."

They both laughed, and then were silent in their own thoughts. Finally, Nic bowed her head and quietly asked.

"Where are they now?"

"Who?"

Jake didn't understand at first, then he did.

"I don't know."

"Is there any way we can find out?"

"Yes, I will have Amanda check on that tomorrow."

"Maybe I can donate or do something to help them."

"I need to get out of here. I didn't realize how late it is."

He began picking up the plates and took them to the kitchen. She followed.

While he rinsed the dishes and she placed them in the dishwasher, he asked.

"If you don't have any plans tomorrow, do you want to go with me to the 911 memorial?"

"Yes, actually I would, I have been meaning to go."

"Great, I will pick you up around two. We can have a late lunch, then go there."

"Don't you have to make reservation?"

"I will take care of that."

"I am having dinner with Madison and Zack tomorrow night, want to join?"

"Sounds great. Do you think it will be okay?"

"Your god child, duh! She will be thrilled, but I will double check if you want."

He reached for his coat.

"You could stay the night. I have a guest room; besides it will be almost daylight by the time you get back to the hotel, you might as well stay."

Jake hesitated. Nicole pointed down the hall.

"Guest room, bathroom, plenty of towel, and supplies. Let me know if you need anything else."

With that she walked up to him, kissed his cheek and turned toward her bedroom. Just as she reached the door she stopped and turned.

"Thanks again for coming over."

He stood there and watched her disappear into her room.

"Don't..."

Finally, he turned and walked into the guest room, closing the door slowly behind him.

Chapter 5

Jake and Winn were in his old jeep racing down the gravel mountain road they had taken many times during their years at UT. They were laughing hard, holding on for dear life, then suddenly, Winn was not driving the jeep but outside staggering toward the car. He was covered in blood shouting at Jake.

"Damnit man, you promised."

Jake jerked awake, his heart pounding out of his skin. Sweat was pouring, handing shaking.

"Shit."

He wiped his face with his arm, lying still in the dark waiting for his heart to slow.

Been a while since he had the nightmare. His dreams started out differently, but always ended the same.

Always with Winn covered in blood, with those wild eyes, always saying the same thing.

"Damnit man, you promised."

Jake flipped off the covers.

"Damn its Winn, I don't remember promising you anything. What the f... are you talking about?"

Slowly, he rose to go to the bathroom. When he returned, he thought he heard a noise.

"Shit, I should have gone home."

He opened the bedroom door and walked silently toward the kitchen, trying to not make any noise. Quietly, he opened the cabinet and reached for a glass. He filled the glass with water and drank, trying to wash away the cotton clogging his throat.

"I am too old for this shit."

Jake downed one more glass before turning toward the bedroom, instead, he stopped and walked into the living room. There he sat in the dark, staring into the great nothingness.

It was past six am.

"What the…?"

Nicole walked into the living room to find her friend sitting on the couch. He was only in his underwear. He appeared to be asleep, but she wasn't for sure. Fear took a quick run through her veins.

"Jake, are you okay?"

She touched his shoulder.

Jake jerked hard. She fell backward ramming into the coffee table. He grabbed for her, and she fell onto the couch on top of him.

It felt like a huge bolt of lightning surging through her body. Skin on skin. It had been a long time. It felt good, it felt bad.

She scrambled to right herself. Her arms flayed as her legs searched for solid footing, as she began sliding off the couch. Frantically, she reached for Jakes leg, instead her arm smashed into his man parts.

"Oh gees."

"Oh god."

"Damn."

He grimaced. Through a jolt of pain, he reached for her, pulling her to him.

She began to laugh uncontrollably. He stared for a moment, then joined in the hysterics.

Suddenly without warning, the sea of tightly sealed emotions broke through. The years of wanting what he must not have, came crashing down. He turned her face to him, as his lips crushed on hers. He began to pull back, but she pushed forward and that was all he needed. The forbidden fruit was right there, right now. All he had to do was take and take he did.

His lips couldn't get enough, his hands couldn't touch enough. He was crazed with want. Jake leaned back onto the couch, bringing her down with him.

Abruptly she stopped, but just long enough to pull at his arm.

In a raspy voice, she whispered.

"Come with me."

He released her long enough for her to stand, then she reached out to him. Quietly, he rose from the couch and followed her. Neither spoke another word. Both laid on her bed; a place where Winston had never been. Nicole reached for Jake's hand, signaling no second thoughts.

He pulled her body to him, taking the gifts she offered. They were both on fire, desperate to reach the top. He pushed, she pulled, he gave, and she took. When she raised up to meet his need, they both carried each other over the edge. It was all consuming, all he had ever wanted wrapped into this one moment.

Nothing in his life had felt like this. Finally, he was where he wanted to be. A place he would have never gone, had his best friend not died. As he lay, trying to catch his breath, he tried to think of what to say. He had to choose his words. She was silent, obviously waiting for him to express his feelings. Everything depended on his words.

Finally, he turned to her, but she was sound asleep. Smiling to himself, he closed his eyes, soon to slumber.

Sometime during the morning, she reached for him, guiding him to her. Once again, they danced the dream of desire. Once again, a tremendous tide of eroticism consumed them. Again, she fell asleep immediately. Jake held her, loving the moment. Pulling her closer to him, his thoughts went to the first time he had laid eyes on her.

During their freshman and sophomore years at the University of Tennessee, both he and Winn enjoyed the attention of many beautiful co-eds. After all they were football stars. There were certain privileges that came their way.

Jake knew about Nicole being Winn's high school sweetheart. But, hell didn't everyone have one of those. He had.

Yet this was college, things were different. They had spent their first two years taking as many offerings as they could handle. There wasn't even a photo of Nicole on his pal's desk.

So, at the beginning of their junior year, when she walked up the sidewalk near the sports dorm where they lived, Jake didn't know she was Winn's Nicole. All he knew was she took his breath away. He shouted and she turned, looked at him, and smiled, then turned back toward the dorm.

He watched her walk away. Her body seemed to be moving in slow motion, like a supermodel, a goddess. He couldn't look away. It was life altering. He watched her disappear into the entrance of the dorm.

At that moment he spotted Winn walking toward him.

"Man, I just saw the future Mrs. Jackson Freeman."

Winn laughed.

"I'm serious man."

He turned to point in the direction of the dorm, when suddenly, Nicole came bouncing out of the front door screaming. The next moment she was Winn's arms, laughing and kissing him.

When Winn introduced her to Jake, he tried to breathe, tried to get his heart out of his throat tried to act normal. That was thirty something years ago. Now he had just made mad passionate love to his dream.

"God Winston."

It was around seven when he woke, she was gone from the bed.
He prayed there were no regrets on her part. He surely didn't have
any. Guilt yes, regrets no. A note on the counter stated she was out
walking Madison's dog, Tank. The offer of coffee and bagels were
there as well. And if he had to leave, she would see him tonight at
Madison's. Hell, he wanted her, not bagels. What happened to them
going to the 911 memorial? Maybe she needed space to process
what they had done.

Jake decided it was best if he took off. He left her a note saying he
would see her tonight. Deciding, maybe giving her time alone
would be the best approach. Tank finally just refused to walk
anymore. He laid down on the sidewalk and looked up at her as if
to say.

"Damn woman, what is your problem? You have dragged
me around these streets for hours, enough already."
Nicole picked up the little Yorkie and cradled him, as she headed
back to the Fetch Club.

"Sweetie, I am so sorry, I didn't mean to walk you to death.
It's just that today, I am in way over my head. You see I made love,
well, had sex last night. Yes, for the first time in over a year, since
Winston."
She rubbed his head vigorously as she continues to walk.

"This is probably more than you want to know, but you see,
last night was the first man besides Winn. Yes, I am forty-eight

86

years old, and this is the second man I have ever been with. Can you believe that?"

Nicole stopped at one of the side parks and ordered a Chai tea, as she continued her conversation with Tank.

"I had forgotten how much I enjoyed it. Winn and I had wonderful times together. It was amazing what we used to do. Well, I shouldn't get into that with you, don't want to embarrass you, but let me just say it was one of our special things in our married life." She sipped her tea, then continued.

"I let that part of me die... at least I thought that part of me was dead... dead and gone... until last night. Then out of nowhere, Jake had sex with me, and I liked it. Am I nuts? I am married to his best friend. Well, was. Why would he do that? Why did he think that was okay? Did he feel sorry for me? Was that pity sex? I don't know what to think, but I do know I liked it. I missed that, and I am embarrassed to say, but pity sex or not, I want more."

She picked up her tea and sat back down.

"Okay, I am going to stop talking now. I know I must be driving you crazy with all this sex talk, after all I am your grandmother."

Tank nuzzled closer as if to say, it's okay, everything is going to be okay.

After dropping Tank off at the Fetch club, Nicole headed home. She was relieved when her apartment was empty. She read the note Jake left.

It simply said see you tonight.

"What is this? What does that mean? What the hell? I am far too old for stupid games. I will find my own way to Madison's. Screw you, Jackson Freeman."

She laughed at that thought.

After taking a shower, Nicole quickly dressed and headed out the door. A cab took her to Police Headquarters. A Mrs. Carmichael, from the HR department had phoned her and asked her to come down and take care of some paperwork.

"This has to be done today for insurance purposes. It is company policy, concerning all of our employees."

Employee, she hadn't even given that a thought. What was she doing?

Mrs. Carmichael was all business, with a bit of attitude thrown in.

"Fill out these forms and give them back to me when you are finished."

She handed over the forms and pointed to a desk across the room.

"Take a seat over there."

Nicole just stood there for a moment, looking down at the forms.

"Is there a problem, do you need a pen or something?"

"No everything is fine, thank you."

Mrs. Carmichael gave her a mean girl stare with extra attitude, until she moved toward the desk.

Nic wanted to say thank you so much for all your kind help, and for making me feel welcome, but of course she didn't. She dug into her purse, found a pen and began. The door opened, and the grey suited man entered. Nicole recognized him from the day before when she bumped into him. He still didn't smile. He joined Mrs. Carmichael behind the counter. They disappeared into her office and closed the door.

Nic thought to herself.

"Well, those two fit."

There were many questions on the form she couldn't fill out, like previous employment, and starting salary, just to name two. She returned the forms back to Mrs. Carmichael.

"Mrs. Roberts, this is incomplete. Who is your superior, what are your hours, and don't you even know your salary? Did they not discuss this with you? Did you take a job without knowing your salary?"

"No, I don't really nee..."

Nicole stopped what she was about to say.

"Well, aren't we special. Regardless, this is unacceptable. Forms have to be filled out."

"I will speak to Mr. Goodhouse and get back with you."

Nicole was beginning to feel that this was a mistake to think she could work at the police department. She had nothing to contribute. She needed to put an end to this, now.

She took the elevator to where the Commissioner's office was. When she spotted Mr. Goodhouse, she asked him if she could speak to the Commissioner.

"He is in a meeting right now. You will have to make an appointment."

He consulted his tablet.

"Perhaps, sometime the first of next week?"

Nic whispered thanks and turned away, her head bowed.

"Nicole, great, you are here. We were just discussing you." She stopped and turned around to see the Commissioner headed toward her. Right behind him was none other than Jake. She glanced at Jake, then quickly back to the Commissioner. She was sure her face was neon red.

"Good Morning Commissioner."

"Now Nicole, I thought we were past the formalities, just Frank, remember?"

She smiled.

"Frank."

"Didn't know you were coming in this morning."

"Mrs. Carmichael called me this morning, to come in and fill out some employment forms."

Frank laughed.

"Oh, those ever-present pesky forms. Look I will have someone take care of that for you. Gary, call down to HR and tell them we will take care of Mrs. Roberts forms"

Jake spoke up.

"Nic, if you are finished, I have a car outside, do you want a ride?"

Once again, she just wanted to get out of there as fast as she could.

"Yes."

Inside of the back seat of the town car, Jake placed his hand on her knee.

"Sweetie, are you okay?"

She stared down at his hand. There was that jolt again.

"Oh God."

She began to talk rapidly.

"Actually no, I'm not okay. Seventy-two hours ago, I was a depressed drunk. Now I am working for the Police Commissioner doing God knows what, and I just had sex with my husband's best friend, not once but three times. I am now a sex crazed depressed drunk."

Jake quickly reached over and punched the button several times to raise the privacy window.

Nic covered her mouth in horror.

"Oh god, I said that out loud, didn't I? Please tell me he didn't hear me."

Jake just smiled and reached for her.

"Oh god, I am so embarrassed."

She buried her head into his shoulders.

In just a few minutes they were at her apartment. He walked with her to the front entrance of the building.

When he began to release her hand, she held on and pulled slightly. He looked at her for a moment, then glanced at his watch. She was about to pull away, when he held up one finger as if to say give me a minute.

Jake walked over to the car and spoke to John, his driver, who laughed and drove away. Jake took Nic's hand and they walked into her building.

They got inside her apartment and walked straight to her bedroom. Once again it was all consuming. The wild desperation to get at each other. They were far from being young, and yet they were acting like it. They couldn't get their clothes off fast enough. It was magic. All-consuming magic.

They both were drenched; both were breathing hard.

"Geez."

She laughed.

He smiled and turned to face her.

"Do you know how amazing you are?"

She kind of laughed.

"I didn't know how you would feel this morning. You know, in the morning light kind of thing. When I woke up and you were gone, I sort of thought you might have had seconds thoughts about you know. I was afraid I had screwed things up."
He played with a strand of her hair as he continued.

"Maybe ruined our friendship, ruined us."

"You are my second."

"What?"

"Winston is the only person I have ever been with my whole life. I met him when I was barely thirteen. We didn't make love until I began college. We did everything else but, you know, stuff, Elvis and Priscilla stuff."

"Oh God, did I hurt you. I was too rough."

"No, not at all, the point I am trying to make is, I trusted Winn completely. Over the years we did some adventurous things, because we both trusted each other. There was so much love and trust."
She lightly touched his arm.

"So, I guess what I am trying to say is I hope I didn't scare you, being too aggressive and all."

"Are you kidding me."

"Well, when you left that short note this morning, I was afraid I had."

"It was heaven to me. You are soooo…"

He grabbed her bottom and squeezed.

"You have me acting crazy."

He rolled on top of her to show just how crazy. She smiled, and they began another dance of afternoon delight, taking each other back to the cliff and jumping off. When they were finished, he laid back on the pillow and cradled her, smiling as he watched her sleep.

So, this is your MO missy. Good to know.

He tried to push thoughts of Winn out of his head, but with no luck.

"I am sorry my brother, I know how much you loved her, and if you were alive you know I would never touch her no matter how much I love her, but you knew didn't you. Even though we never spoke of it, you always knew, God Winston. You never asked what happened to that girl I said I was going to marry. You just kept trying to fix me up, until I finally gave in and married Mary, in part to get you off my back. God knows I didn't love her, and we know what a complete disaster that was, totally my fault. For five long years I barely went through the motions. It wasn't fair to her. I am glad she found somebody else to love her. She is happy now. Winn, Mary knew…she knew. The last thing she said to me after we signed the divorce papers…You are a sad man, Jackson Freeman. You will never have her; you know that don't you. As long as Winston is on this earth, you can only be her friend. God, Winn, I never said a word to anyone, but she knew, just as you knew."

94

Jake looked over at Nic sleeping soundly. He had to get up, he had a meeting to attend. He wanted to stay where he was all afternoon, but some very important scientists were probably already on their way to the Waldorf. He had to get going or he would be late. He eased out of bed and headed to the shower. Once dressed, he wrote a long note letting her know how much he enjoyed their day together, and he would pick her up around 6:30 pm to go to Madison's for dinner. He drew a heart on the sheet of paper, something he had never done before in his life. Jake left the apartment, making sure the door was locked from the inside.

Six-thirty on the dot, Nicole buzzed Jake up. She laughed as she opened the door for him.

"Is this time thing going to be an issue with you, because you have to know I am a girly girl. Time is just a number."

He couldn't help himself, he grabbed her and swung her in his arms.

"Not a problem, however, this might be."

He couldn't believe how randy he was.

"I can't show up at Madison's like this."

She laughed.

"Well, I guess we will just have to stay at least six feet apart. Do you think that will work, or … we could just take care of business now so to speak?"

"Woman you are bad."

He grabbed for her. Soon they were on the bed.

Afterwards there was no sleeping, no lingering. Quickly, they showered and dressed. As they walked into Madison's lobby, they were giggling like teenagers. Madison hugged them and headed to the kitchen where Luke and Tank were.

The evening was festive, the food was amazing. Nic and Madison cleaned the kitchen, then joined the men to watch the Giants football game. All four were Giants fans, mostly because Eli was Peyton Manning's little brother. It didn't matter what jersey Peyton wore, they loved him. He played for the University of Tennessee. Nicole marveled at how quickly she and Winston jumped from the Colt's bandwagon to be a Broncos' fan. Probably took about 6 seconds.

Later, when they were walking to the town car, a man and two woman approached Jake, asking if they could get a selfie with him. The women flirted and giggled. When they finally gave up the flirt and went away, barely acknowledging Nic's presence, she couldn't help but to tease Jake.

"You know I almost forgot just how famous you are Senator. Do you get this often, I bet you do? I bet you have to fight them off. Glad I didn't get between you and the eager two, I think I might have been crushed."

She laughed, he didn't. He grabbed her hand.

"You know I would never let anyone hurt you, right?" Soon they were at her apartment. There wasn't even a discussion. He stayed the night.

Next morning as they shared breakfast, Jake brought up last night again.

"Nic, sometimes folks take pictures of me when I least expect it, or even when I don't know it. Sometimes, these pictures get into papers or on the internet. Now for me, I wouldn't mind one bit. Hell, being seen with you could only give me street credit. You are so beautiful, and smart... god."

He stopped talking and just stared at her for a moment.

"I know you have concerns about Madison."

Nic put up her hand.

"As far as what we do here, it is no one's business, and we will just have to be discrete when we are in public. Madison knows about us going out to functions. She is okay with it."

She put her hand on his.

"It will be okay."

Jake knew better, he would talk about it more later.

"Nic, I have had a great time with you this week. It has been amazing. More than you could ever know. But I have to fly back to Washington tomorrow. I don't want to, but duty calls. I want this, what we have started to continue. I'd like to come back soon."

She smiled and said.

"I would like that."

Shortly afterwards, Jake was on his way to his meeting and she was on her way to the Fetch Club for Tank.

She could have sworn she saw a note of hesitation in her grand puppy. Still he came forward, tail wagging.

Once outside, she began explaining herself.

"I am sorry about yesterday. I promise no more crazed ranting. Let's go to Battery Park, okay."

Chapter 6

Enhanced language abilities, that's what the doctors called it. The fact that she could not only hear but understand so many different languages made this an easy adventure. Fortunately for Nic, she could turn her hearing capabilities on and off when she chose.

Quickly, she moved from one to another group listening for trigger words. In one of the meetings, Mr. Thomas talked about the list of trigger words. Words of interest for the newly formed NYC task force and Homeland Security.

He told her the list was on her new laptop.

"This list is constantly updated so check it often."

This was her god given gift, now after all these years she was finally using it.

Nic thought she heard something from three men standing next to the police memorial. One spoke in anger using a Turkic dialect. She moved closer to the wall of honor and leaned down pretending to be interested in a specific name. She pulled Tank closer, and touched one of the names, running her fingers gently over it, while continuing to listen.

She heard trigger words spoken by the group, she was sure of it. Quickly, she led Tank away from the area back to the Fetch Club.

Once home, she removed her brand new tripped-out scrambled apple laptop from its brand-new leather case.

"Okay, let's see if I am right about these triggers."

It only took a few minutes of browsing. Bingo!

Now what was she supposed to do with this information. She had no idea. Since she hadn't told them she was planning on going out looking for trigger words, no one had a plan for her.

She was intimidated by most of the people over at One Police Plaza. They had not been very nice to her, not mean, just not especially nice.

"Nic, quit being such a southerner."

She was getting a big dose of reality. When she helped with the Memphis City School programs, or did charitable work, the men and women basically gushed over her talents. She was very appreciated. Now she was just a worker bee. No one knew her skills, or really gave a damn. This was a job, big difference.

"Okay, here goes nothing."

She picked up the phone and dialed their number.

"May I speak to a uuhhhh... Mr. Thomas?"

"Well, does this Mr. Thomas have a first name?"

She knew it two-seconds ago, why hadn't she written it down.

"Oh sorry, let me look."

Nic heard a deep sigh, then the words please hold.

After a few minutes, she just knew she had been placed in no man's land. She couldn't blame her; she had forgotten the man's first name. Perhaps she should have asked for the department, then she realized she didn't know that either.

"Oh great, just great."

She finally hung up.

"Well, shit."

At that moment the phone rang, it was Jake.

"I am getting into the car now. Are you still up for a late lunch?"

"I just got back from walking Tank; can you maybe pick something up. We can eat here. I still have to take a shower."

He laughed and said.

"Your wish is my command, be there in a few."

The bottom dropped out of her heart.

She whispered into the phone.

"Oh, God, please, please be careful."

He had already hung up.

She barely made it to the porcelain in time. She threw up until there was nothing left. Her body shook.

"Damn, damn."

She turned the shower on and step in. Minutes later, she stepped out, reached for the towel, then headed for the kitchen for a glass of wine.

By the time she dressed, Jake was at the door. She buzzed him in.

"I scored us the most amazing food. At least it smells like it. My driver, John took me to his cousin's food truck."

He took one look at her and put the sacks on the kitchen counter.

Nic was sitting on the couch downing her glass of wine. Her hands were shaking.

He took the glass of wine from her and placed it on the coffee table, then knelt next to her.

"Your wish is my command, be there in a few. That was the last words Winston ever said to me. The exact words."

"Oh gees, baby. That was something Winston's dad used to say all the time, guess we picked it up. I am sorry, I didn't know."

She looked down at him.

"Of course, you didn't. It just hit me; I am so stupid sometimes."

She started laughing over her tears.

"Did I hear you say something about lunch? I am starving."

He gave her a long look, then rose and went into the kitchen.

There was so many layers to this woman.

He grabbed another glass and went back into the living room. It was way early for him, but hell, he wasn't going to let her drink alone.

She looked over at her new apple laptop and immediately began feeling guilty.

"Oh gees, I left that thing on. I am probably in big trouble."

She walked over and shut it down.

"I was out and about with Tankie. I wanted to try my luck at listening again. This time on purpose. I wanted to see what would happen if I actually tried to eavesdrop. I can't get those girls out of my mind. I need to do something to help. We went down to the park, and you know what, it was a whole lot easier than I expected." She turned and pointed to the laptop.

"I overheard some men talking, using some of the trigger words they told us about. Jake I actually heard three. Okay, so now what do I do. I have no earthly idea what to do with this information. Who should I contact? And to be honest, those people over at Police headquarters scare me."

She crossed over to the couch, sat down and smiled at him.

Dark thoughts cloud his mind for a brief moment, but when she smiled at him, he pushed them away.

"Well, they do."

She threw up her hands.

He couldn't help but laugh.

"Okay, smarty pants, what do I do?"

"Well, do you mind if I give it a shot?"

"Please do."

They both smiled at each other. He picked up his phone, hit speed dial, and winked at her. The Commissioner picked up immediately.

Nic sat quietly and listened to Jake do his thing. Over the years, when she was married to Winston, Jake seem to sit back and quietly cheer his best friend on. In her mind, Jake was always Winston's sidekick.

But now she was watching a totally different Jake, a man very much in charge. She watched him tell the Police Commissioner of New York City what he wanted done. At one-point Nic stopped listening to the spoken word and just watched.

When he hung up, he turned to her and smiled once again. She didn't say a word, just stared at him for a moment, and then rose from the couch. He was confused. She walked to the hall and turned. She began unbuttoning her blouse slowly.

"If the honorable Senator from the great state of Tennessee knew just how turned on I was at this moment, he would not be sitting in that chair."

With that she disappeared to her bedroom.

"Dammmnnn!"

When he walked into the room, she pushed him onto the bed and began.

He was no dummy, he raised his arms and rested them on the back of his head and watched in unbelievable wonder. God, what he had dreamed about, all his desires and dreams were coming true.

It was the most amazing experience of love making in his life. It wasn't just sex; it was pure heaven. Since laying eyes on this beautiful woman so many years ago, this was his forbidden desire. And now he watched and felt as she made her way up his body.

Finally, it was his turn to participate, and he did. His life was finally coming together. It was finally making sense. They took each other to that special place so few get to go. It took several moments to breathe normally again. He wanted to tell her how he felt, had always felt. His heart was so wrapped up, but she was fast asleep. He wrapped her into him and slept.

Her cell phone buzzed a text from Madison. She replied, then turned and headed to the bathroom.

He headed to the showers as well. After getting dressed, he walked into the living room where she was sitting on the couch, tapping away on her laptop.

"Perfect timing. I just finished rechecking my report. Did they tell you where I am supposed to send this?"

He pulled out his cell phone and joined her on the couch.

"Yes, Frank gave me a secure email address to send your info. Here it is."

As she typed, he repeated his conservation with the Commissioner.

"He said if you have any questions, call..."

He consulted his phone again.

"Ahhh, here it is, Mr. Jason Thomas. He said you met him the other day. Any way, he is in charge. And Frank said if you can't reach Mr. Thomas and it is an emergency, just call him. Here let me have your phone, and I'll put these numbers in for you."

He finished and handed her phone back.

"I put them in your favorites so it will be easier to find. Now shall we eat. I am staving."

Nic hopped up off the couch.

"Yes, it smelled fabulous when you brought it in. I bet it is still tasty."

As they enjoyed their food, they talked about the task force.

"I don't know if I'm supposed to show you or not, but I don't care, you got me into this, so I think you should see what is on my fancy convert machine. She showed him all the programs."

The trigger words program was the one that interested her the most. As she told him about it, her eyes lit up. There was energy in her voice. She no longer seemed to doubt herself. Jake watched as the dark seem to move away, leaving only light surrounding her.

He was happy for her, for himself, happy they were together. The euphoria of it all pushed away any sobering thoughts of the danger she might be putting herself in. It was close to midnight when they began to clear the dishes.

He wasn't for sure if he should stay the night again, wasn't for sure if she wanted him to. Jake walked over and picked up his coat.

"Aren't you going to stay?"

He stared down at her, then laid his coat down.

Quietly he spoke.

"Yes."

Jake reached for her, kissing her gently, then holding her close.

She finally pulled away.

"Jake, thank you for taking time off from what I imagine is an extremely busy schedule, to come be with me."

Tears formed in her eyes.

"Since Winston's death, I have been in a free fall. Every day, everything has become dark and heavy. For over a year I have been basically just going through the motions. Lately even that has become increasingly more difficult."

She would never tell him or anyone else just how dark and desperate things had become.

"Since you came, it's not been so dark and heavy. Thank you"

She wiped the tears and continued.

"I know you are Winston's friend, and you certainly didn't have to come to New York to try and fix me, but you did. For that I will always be grateful."

Nic walked over to turn off the side lamp.

"I think I am crawling out of that deep hole. I am not so sad anymore. You don't have to worry about me now."

As she turned off the last lamp, she said.

"What kind of friend am I to keep you up so late when you have an early flight?"

The hammer of her words crushed at his heart. Didn't she know, how could she not know?

He just stood there and stared at her.

"Jake, would you stay?"

Her words said she would be okay, but her sad eyes were telling a different story. He didn't say anything, couldn't, instead, he just followed her to the bed. Nic snuggled up against him and was asleep within minutes. He placed his arm around her and laid in the dark. Soon he slept. The morning light came too soon.

He dressed quickly. His driver would be downstairs momentarily. He wrote her a long note, said too much, wadded up the paper and started over. Time was up, he had to leave. He placed the new note on the counter and eased out the door.

Back at the hotel, he showered, dressed, packed, and was on his way to the airport in less than an hour.

There was so much business to take care of. He had let things pile up while in New York. The Senator spent his flight time catching up. He went through one issue after another with amazing speed. This was his gift, his talent. Nicole had her gift, he had his. Jake had always been able to go through piles of information quickly deciphering what was important and what was not. This was the gift that helped in the Senate. It also was the gift that helped him become a wealthy man, long before he entered politics.

Jake was around eleven years old when he was first introduced to the possibilities of making money through the world of wall street. One of his teachers from the orphanages he grew up in taught him the fundamentals. He made a deal with Jake.

If he helped Professor Edwards after school, he would pay him money to invest in the stock market. He told Jake he would show him how to invest. Of course, the professor put in more funds than Jake earned by doing chores.

He never forgot the day Mr. Edwards showed him how much he had made when one of the stocks split. That was the beginning. Mr. Edwards helped him open a bank account as well as a stock account.

To Jake, the Professor was the dad he never had. Jake was one of the lucky ones thanks to Mr. Edwards. So many in orphanages have a pretty hard time of it when they age out, but Jake had Professor Edwards, and until his death, they remained close. Jake made sure that the Professor wanted for nothing.

Mr. Edward saw a special something in Jake. And for that he would be forever grateful for it was that gift that made Jake a billionaire before he was forty. He also used that gift to help his best friend Winston.

He leaned back for a moment and closed his eyes, remembering the time Winston came to him several months after they had graduated from UT.

"Jake, man I am drowning. A wife, a baby, and a shit job I hate. This is not what I envisioned for myself. You were smart not to get saddled with so much before you had a chance to establish yourself."

Winn looked up at Jake and quickly corrected himself.

"Hey man, don't get me wrong. I love Nic and Madison, but I am in over my head. I barely make ends meet. My credit cards are maxed out and if it wasn't for my dad, I would be in deeper trouble. I can't just keep going to him."

Jake offered him another beer, and over the next several hours he helped his friend come up with a plan.

Jake offered him a loan to pay off his credit cards. Then showed him how to manage his finances. Winston stuck with the plan and was able to pay Jake back over the next year and half.

With the last payment, they celebrated together. Jake then offered him a business opportunity. A few months later, on June 1, 1985, Winston opened his first sports bar. He named it WINN. Besides his family, Winston's great love was sports. He turned his love into a chain of successful sports bars throughout the SEC south.

Over the years he added sports clothing, a shoe line, and a sports drink. Last, but certainly, the most lucrative was a sports agency, representing the best of the SEC and professional players.

Everything was under the name Winn Enterprises. Jake was his silent partner, who took care of the financial part. Winston ran the everyday operations and was very good at it. The business grew. Jake's gamble on his best friend paid off.

Together they made a lot of money. But the real wealth came from investments Jake made. He was a genius at picking the right stocks, buying into the right real estate or other opportunities when they came up. It was his gift. Jake made sure his buddy Winn got in on some of the less risky opportunities when they became available.

Winn was a multi-millionaire, but Jake was a multi-billionaire. To this day, Nic didn't know about Jake's involvement in their investments, no need. When he was elected into the Senate his investments went into a blind trust. Winn's funds were set up to be completely separate from Jakes. Their partnership was dissolved. Winston never told Nicole of their financial involvement. Under the circumstances he wouldn't have either.

The only thing that he still had his name on was the trust set up for Madison, right after she was christened. That was his present to her as her godparent. With Jake's financial knowledge, the trust had grown tremendously over the years, making Madison a wealthy young woman. She did know all about the trust. When she turned eighteen, Winston and Jake went over everything with her. He still was the executer of the trust; however, it would be transferred to her when she turns 32.

Chapter 7

Finally, Jake was home, but this time home wasn't quite the same. His usual sanctuary was not so much. He made himself a drink then picked up his phone and dialed her number. No answer, disappointed, he left a message.

Nic and Tank headed back to Battery Park for another round of snooping.

"Tankster, I don't like the idea of thinking we are being nosey, so why don't we call ourselves spies."

She giggled and he barked.

"Alrighty then, it's official, we are spies."

As they walked around, she noticed the same men from yesterday. They spoke the same Turkic language saying pretty much the same as before. At one point, she felt their eyes on her. Quickly she turned and led Tank in the opposite direction, then headed home.

This time she took her grand puppy with her. She just didn't want to be alone. Madison and Zack were more than happy for Tank to have a sleep over at grandma's place. After feeding him, she pulled out the laptop and began typing her report. Thanks to Jake she had no problems sending the information.

She closed her eyes and thought of Jake, and their time together the past few days. What a surprise he had been. She felt her body heat up when her thoughts went to what they had done. Never in a million years, did she think they would be having sex. And not just sex, but amazing, can't get enough kind of sex. A sudden massive wave of guilt sweep over her.

"Oh Winn, I am so sorry, I miss you so much, how could I have done that to you, and with Jake of all people."

She rose and made her way to the kitchen, poured a glass of wine then turned to the couch. Tank was on the couch waiting for her.

She picked up her cell, then settled back, rubbing Tank's head. She noticed Jake had called. She hit the return button.

"Hi there, Glad you made it home safe and sound."

"Yes, I did."

Jake smiled as he sat on his couch.

"I had a great time in New York, with you."

"Me too, that was an unexpected surprise, an amazing one, but still a surprise."

They both laughed into their phones.

They were creating that atmosphere … the one when two people are super charged with wonder. The one that makes the heartbeat faster, makes one feel alive, no matter how old you are.

"I have been going through my rather large pile of mail. Just opened a 'Save the Date' invitation from the White House. It is for a state dinner the end of April honoring the President of France. And guess what, Bruce Springsteen is going to perform for the event. If I recall, he is one of your favorites, want to be my plus one?"

"Oh my god, are you serious?"

He laughed

"Yes, I am serious."

"Well, you had me at White House dinner, but on the off chance that I could actually meet The Boss. What can I say but Wow?"

She giggled.

"He is on my bucket list you know."

"Bucket list?"

"Yeah, the list of things you want to do before you die."

"You want to do Bruce Springsteen?"

"No, of course not."

She laughed, then cleared her throat.

"Well, actually yes. He was my hall pass, you know, the one person married people can have sex with given the opportunity. Let me see, Winn's was, well at first it was Michelle Pfeiffer, but he kept changing his, next it was Sandra Bullock, then I can't remember."

She laughed again.

"But I stayed with Bruce. I was steadfast."

Even through the phone Jake could sense she was going down memory lane. After a moment she continued.

"And you are throwing in a couple of really good-looking Presidents, how could a girl say no?"

"There will probably be a few more folks invited that you might find interesting."

"Like who? Give me names."

"Oh, probably a whole bunch of Senators, and a celebrity of three… then there is me. I will be there."

"Oh yes, there is that… you."

They both laughed.

Then guilt reared its head.

"Jake, I have to go, Madison is texting me."

"Okay, I will call you tomorrow."

Jake hung up; he knew in his heart Madison had not texted her. But he understood. He could hear the guilt in her voice, perhaps because he felt it too. Man, how do people have affairs?

He rose from his couch, picked up his drink and walked out onto the patio. It was freezing outside, but he hardly felt it.

"Dammit Winn, if you were still here, I would never do anything, never, you know that. I would respect that forever; you know that man."

He balled his fist and banged it against the patio rail.

"But you left us, you left her. I know you didn't mean too, but you did."

Jake finished off his drink and turned to go back inside.

"I am sorry man, but it's my turn now."

He whispered to himself

"My turn now, damn it."

Just as he sat back down at his desk, his phone rang.

"Hello."

"Yes, this is Senator Freeman."

Jake listened for a minute.

"Wow, does she know yet? No, I will call her. What time is the meeting scheduled? I will let her know."

Jake grabbed a pen and pad and jotted down the information.

"Okay, and thanks for calling. Keep me posted. I want any updates immediately, thanks David."

With the commissioner's blessing, Jake had asked David Johnson, one of the members of the task force Nic was involved with to keep him appraised about what was happening especially if it involved her. So far, some Knick's court side tickets and a couple front row seat concerts had made his new friend David quite happy. One of the perks of being a U. S. Senator is freebies to just about any event imaginable.

He quickly dialed Nic's number.

A sleepy voice answered

"Oh, did I wake you?"

"Just resting my eyes, what's going on?"

"Well, it looks like you did it again. The Intel you gathered proved to be important. The task force raided a facility this evening. They confiscated a number of weapons, money, drugs, etc., plus some unsavory characters bent on doing harm to New York."

"Were there any girls? Did they save them?"

"I don't think there was any human trafficking this time." Jake cleared his throat.

"They want you to meet with them tomorrow morning. They will have a car for you at 9 am. Can you make that?"

"Yes, I think so, shall I call to confirm?"

"I have to call them back anyway, so I can let them know."

"Okay."

They talked another minute then said goodnight.

Nic woke Tank to tell him about what Jake had said.

"Looks like we are pretty good at this spy stuff. Who would have thunk it, you and me, protectors of the American Way?"

She stood up and began to dance.

"Looks like a bird, a plane, no, it's super woman and her faithful companion, Tankster."

She laughed hard as she hugged the little guy.

After over a year she was finally beginning to enjoy being alive.

"Winn, I hope it is okay. I still miss you so much, but I think maybe I am climbing out of the darkness. I love you Winn, I will always love you."

She poured herself a glass of water and opened her covert laptop. She looked for the updated trigger word list. She also checked out other programs such as human trafficking, and terrorist groups. She was particularly interested in gathering research on human trafficking, and what is being done about it. A couple of hours later she closed her laptop, picked up the little Yorkie and headed to bed.

The next morning, Nic smiled as she glanced at her watch. Tank had already been picked up and was on his way to the Fetch Club, she was dressed and waiting for the car.

"Jake's time thing must be rubbing off on me."

At the meeting, they asked her none-stop questions for about twenty minutes. Questions about the location of the group, what was said, and descriptions of the men, etc., etc., then Mr. Thomas said.

"Thank you, Mrs. Roberts for coming in to meet with us. What you did took courage and we appreciate it; however, you cannot go off on your own like that again. There are dangers to what you are doing. I repeat, you must be careful. From now on, you must coordinate with me. Do you understand?"

He just stared at her for a moment.

"There are rules in place we must follow. It is for everyone's protection... everyone's."

Jason Thomas had just come from a meeting with the committee members in the conference room. He had strongly voiced his opposition to what she was doing.

"Do you realize how dangerous this is? This has disaster written all over it. All that proposed Homeland Security windfall will suddenly disappear if anything happens to the Senator's special friend."

But no one seemed to be listening. Everyone was too wrapped up in the win to think it through. He would talk to the Commissioner one on one later, but for now he had work to do.

"What we have discussed in this meeting should be kept confidential for everyone's safety. No one is to mention Mrs. Roberts name, or anyone else's for that matter. What is said in here, stays in here, is that understood?"

One thing he was able to do before he met with Nicole and the group was make sure the paper trail concerning her and one PP was erased. Since she insisted on not drawing a salary, it wasn't difficult to delete her information. It would protect both the department and her.

He gave a nod toward his assistant, to hand out the packet.

"In each packet is an iPhone. It is a smaller iPhone than what you are used to, however, it is equipped with so much more. This will be everyone's point of communication. Use this phone only... let me repeat... this phone only for any task force communications, and do not use it for anything else. All you must do is hit the on button and you are connected immediately to our center. Until further notice, always keep this phone with you. Mrs. Roberts, that means you as well. It is GPS connected."

He stopped for a moment and looked at everyone.

"Any questions? If not, let's get back to work. Mrs. Roberts your car is waiting for you."

Mr. Thomas looked down to consult his papers.

"The same driver that drove you here will pick you up. Mr. Daniels is his name. Anytime you are picked up by Police Headquarers, you will be given the name of your driver and his or her photo ahead of time. Make sure the ID matches before you get into the car. Is that clear to you and everyone else in this room?"

He put down his paper and gave her a stern look.

"Thank you again and remember do not say a word to anyone outside this room. And always keep your phone with you, understood?"

She nodded and left the room. She slipped on her coat and walked outside. The wind whipped around the corner of the building.

"I wonder if it is ever going to be warm again?"

She tried to draw her coat closer to her, as she turned to search for her town car. Once again, she saw the grey suited man walking briskly in front of her. She watched as a black van pulled up beside him. The door automatically opened, and he climbed in.

Her town car pulled up near her. The driver got out and held out his ID then he held the door open or her. She gave him her address, then slipped into the back seat. She let out a big sigh and said to herself.

"Well, alrighty, very cloth and dagger of you, Mr. Thomas." She checked her own phone for messages. One call was from Danielle Perry, and one from Jake. She chose Jake.

"Hi, you, how did it go?"

"Okay I guess, they asked me a lot of questions, then gave me a packet with a phone and stuff and then dismissed me. I am on my way home now. I am not supposed to mention any of this to anyone, except you of course. Well, I didn't actually ask anyone if it was all right to talk to you."

"Yes, of course, tell me everything."

"Well, since you got me into this, yeah, you got me into this mess, then you leave town, leaving me to fend for myself, mister." She chuckled softly.

"Wish I was there; we could go play and stuff."
Nic giggled at her thoughts.

"Now Ms. Nic, you need to get your mind out of the gutter. I meant go to a museum or a seminar or stuff."

"Senator, you have to be present for stuff to be going on."

"Well, not necessary, haven't you heard of phone stuff?"

"You are a very bad man Senator."

They both laughed.

"I am home now."

"Okay, I will give you a call later."

"I would like that."

Once in her apartment, she slipped out of her coat, grabbed a Diet Pepsi and settled on her couch. She took a sip then opened her packet. Along with the phone came a sheet of instructions. This was getting kind of crazy. She looked at the clock, it was noon, and she hadn't eaten yet. She should eat, but she wasn't hungry. She could feel the dark clouds forming in her soul. She grabbed her head and squeezed it hard.

"No, damnit, I am not going back there again."

Quickly, she grabbed her coat and left the apartment. Once she had Tank on a leash, they headed toward the doggie park. Mindlessly, she tossed the tennis ball for the pup to chase. She was not going back down the dark hole again. She just couldn't. Still restless, she attached Tanks leash and headed toward the river. As they walked she listened for more trigger words but heard none. Nic was well aware of what Mr. Thomas had said to her, but she was into this now. If she could help save young girls and boys, then so be it. After a while she returned Tank to the Fetch Club.

Back in her apartment, she rode her bike hard for an hour, then showered. She was getting the shakes, she had to eat something. She arranged a plate of cheese and crackers with some grapes and celery and made herself eat. She opened the laptop and began her research. Something had clicked within her as she typed ideas about what she wanted to do.

After listening to Mr. Thomas at the meeting this morning, she realized she needed to take steps to make things safer for herself and her dog. Being a dog walker was a perfect excuse to be in the parks or anywhere for that matter. New Yorkers were so used to dogs, they hardly notice. But the thought of putting Tank in possible danger was unacceptable. She would have to come up with another plan. She would sign up to walk other dogs.

Another part of her plan was to find out where the hot spots were, where these groups gathered. She would do research on that without the task force knowing about it. She could develop her own disguises for her own safety. It was exhilarating to be putting a plan together. She was in the moment when the phone rang, she jumped.

"Hi there."

She spoke quickly.

"Jake, I have been putting together a plan of how to proceed with what I have been doing."

He could hear the excitement in her voice. He just listened. After a few minutes it hit him. My god, what have I done. Why had he not realized? He should have never let this get stated in the first place. He had not been completely honest with Nicole. Weeks ago, at the initial meeting with the Commissioner, Jake had mentioned what Nic had overheard. He used it to emphasis the fact that being a newcomer to the city, she didn't know what to do with the information. He used it for his own agenda. But when the Commissioner kept asking questions about Nicole and her language skills, he went into a full mode sales pitch. Jake offered future favors for a present one. Any politician worth their salt knew how to use the favor card. It was how the game was played. Being on the Homeland Security Committee made it easy.

The New York Homeland Security Department as well as the police department wanted more federal money for their annual budget. Ever since Nic had moved to NYC he had focused on getting more funds designated to the city. As bad as that might sound, it was simply the truth. Nicole and not New York, was his main reason he fought for so hard for the extra funds. So, he used the more funds planned, plus strongly suggested there would be more to come for NYC, if Frank could perhaps find a position for Nicole.

Frank got the message loud and clear. He suggested he meet with Nicole, thus, the invite to Madison's event. Jake didn't feel bad about it because he was sure once the Commissioner met Nicole, he would be on board to offer her a position on the newly formed task force.

All be it, in the Commissioner's words, a fluff position, but it would be a place for her to go. A place beside her tiny apartment where she spent too much time in darkness. He wanted to help her, and he had accomplished that, but he hadn't thought it through.

However, when her language skills picked up another conversation that had been instrumental in apprehending some more very bad people, things changed. Suddenly, she was an asset, doing good work for the department. They were wrapped up in the win, and he was so wrapped up in her, he hadn't thought about the danger. She was supposed to be in house, setting up language programs, not roaming the streets looking for bad men. It was dangerous, and it could get her killed, if he didn't stop her.

He tried to listen, but his mind kept jumping. Winston would kill him if anything happened to her. He had screwed up, but he would come up with something that would fix this.

"Jake, are you still there?"

"Yes,   sorry   for   the   interrupt."
He sighed, then spoke softly.

"Tell me again."

"I was just saying that for the first time in a long time, I am finding a purpose. For most of my life I have been a wife and mother. Madison doesn't need me anymore... as it should be, and Winston."

She swallowed.

"Winston is gone. But, thanks to you, I am finding my purpose again. You are a good friend Jackson Freeman."

"You know it is almost the weekend. How bout I fly up? A friend of mine has been telling me about this fabulous new restaurant I think he said it was in the meat packing district. Meant to try it out while I was in town last time, but somehow, I got distracted. Maybe you can make it up to me."

"Well, first-of-all it is just Wednesday. Besides that, I would love it, if you can get away again."

"Hey, I am the boss around here. They can't fire me, at least not for another year or so. I will email you my itinerary. I have to go to a meeting; I will give you a call when I am through."
He immediately buzzed for his assistant.

"Amanda, would you book me a flight to New York Friday afternoon. Move whatever appointments you need to."
He rose from his desk and began pacing.

"Oh, find me a great restaurant that has recently opened in New York, preferably in the Meat Packing District. It needs to be cool and make reservations for two. Also, I need a gift, not the usual, this needs to be something special, discrete but special. Plus, get that private security group we used last year; you remember the one. Thanks Amanda."

She just looked at him and eased out of his office. Well, well Romeo, glad to see you are back in the saddle, it's been awhile. I knew there was something going on. Surely hope this one is worth it. She looked up the security company's number and made the call.

Once Jake got off the phone with the security company, he felt a little better. He hired them right away. They were to start immediately. He would meet them this weekend. It would cost him, but keeping her safe was probably, hell it was the most important thing in his life. If anything, ever happened to her...

Chapter 8

She knew sleep would evade her tonight. She watched a movie, went to bed, got up and now she was pacing. Finally, out of desperation, she poured herself a glass of wine, then pulled out her covert laptop as she called it. She named it Verdi. The last time she had opened it, she had noticed some programs available to her. She took a large gulp of wine and began.

"Well, Miss Verdi let's see what you've got."
Nic went straight to the subject of human trafficking. The more she read the more horrified she became. She had no idea. How can the world not be more outraged about this?
Tears formed in her eyes, as she grabbed a tissue.

Modern slavery generates approximately 50 Billion dollars in profits each year. According to research the U. S. State Department estimates about 800,000 people are traded across state and international borders each year. Eighty percent of the victims are women and girls. More than two-thirds of them are sold into the sex trade business. On and on she read about the horrors that are forced upon young girls and boys. She also learned about people being sold into slavery for so many other reasons. Domestic, farm, land, seamstresses, and so much more. The new trend is to take younger students for their computer skills. Hacking is the new terrorists' trend.

There would be no sleep tonight. Nicole began forming a plan. With-in three hours she had written a twelve-page white paper on ideas of what could be done to combat this horror.

Finally, fatigue sat in. She finally closed her laptop and went to bed. Still her head was spinning with information. Her mind wouldn't shut off. She got out of bed and did some yoga moves. It was around 5 am when she crawled back into bed. Finally, she slept.

While Nicole slumbered, a large room in a building located in one of the seedier areas of Brooklyn was buzzing with activity. Several boys were busy on their computers. However, the young students were not researching papers to further their education. Instead they were researching ways to hack into security systems of governments around the world, mainly the United States. Some of the young men were tasked to review what was happening within the social networking systems. Looking for anything that would help their cause.

"Mom, mom, are you here? Oh, there you are. Are you okay? Is something wrong?"

Madison sat on her mom's bed and felt her forehead.

"You don't seem to have fever."

Through her grogginess Nicole began to realize what was going on.

"Oh baby, did I scare you. Sorry I forgot to text you back last night. I got adsorbed in research on my computer. I was up reading most of the night. Went to bed around daylight."

"When you didn't text last night, and I couldn't get you this morning, I got worried. Do you know it's almost two pm?" Madison stood up and paced.

"God mom, don't scare me like this."

"I am so sorry baby."

Madison waited while her mom showered and dressed, then they went for a late lunch. It was nice being with her daughter. Nicole couldn't help herself; she told her daughter a little of what she was doing at One PP. She shared her new purpose. Today, they were two grown-ups sharing their thoughts, their dreams, not just mother and daughter. It was rare, it was fun.

Nic felt bad that she scared her daughter, however, she was enjoying this rare undivided attention.

After lunch, they shopped. Both Madison and Nicole were loaded down with bags of goodies. She had treated her daughter to a shopping spree. It was so worth it. By the time she returned to her apartment, she felt happy, renewed. She had purchased warm clothes, and good boots for walking around Manhattan in winter. After storing her new purchases, she changed to comfy clothes, and climbed onto the couch.

Guilt came over her as she looked at calls on her cell. She had not returned Ms. Perry's phone calls. Before she could talk herself out of it, she punched return.

"Ms. Perry, I am sorry for the delay in returning your call. I have taken on another project that suddenly presented itself. Thank you so much for taking the time to meet with me."

Ms. Perry was still the diplomat she had been when they had first met. Nic said goodbye and that was that.

She felt bad, just not quite so much.

Now what was she going to do with the rest of the day. She had to keep busy. She was still terrified of what she had done that one night. Minutes later she was out in the cold with her new duds on. Everything was warmer, and her new boots were made for long walks. It took about twenty minutes to reach the costume store she had found online. She browsed for a while, until she came upon what she was looking for. She bought a couple of vintage outfits, head to toe. She would purchase more another time, but this was a good start. Next, she visited the pet store just a few doors down.

She lingered there just watching the dogs. There would be time later to decide what to do about that. Nicole picked up take-out food from a Chinese restaurant she came across on her way home. First thing she did was text Madison. She wouldn't make that mistake again.

Madison picked up the phone and dialed her godfather. She tried to remain calm. It had been hard to wait until after she finished work, to call him.

"Hi sweetie, what a nice surprise."

"What is my mother into?"

Madison didn't waste words.

"Uncle Jake, did you know what my mom is doing? She is out on the streets hunting down terrorists. Did you know that? This is beyond crazy. She can't do that, nobody does that. This is insane."

The longer she spoke the higher her voice became.

"You have to stop her, you have to!"

Jake took a deep breath.

"Yes, baby, I know that. When I arranged this job for her, I had no idea she would take it so far. I thought she could help with the language skill area. Frank wants her to design programs and instruct recruits."

"One day, she accidentally overheard some men talking in Russian. That was about a month ago. She was instrumental in helping capture a human trafficking group. And a few days ago, she did it again. She overheard a second group, but this time it was no accident, this time she went searching for them."

"Uncle Jake you have to promise me you will protect my mom. You must. I don't know what I would do if I lost her too. You have to stop her."

"I know baby, I know."

After they hung up, Jake poured himself a stiff drink. He would have to come up with something that would stop her, without her knowing it. He had to keep her safe. He would fix this, he had to.

Nic had a good day. Being with her daughter had given her that something that only a parent could understand. It was almost eleven pm, and she felt like going to bed.

"Hi you."

"Hope I am not calling too late. Just got home. Long day at the office."

"Guess the business of running the government requires a lot."

"You know what, it really shouldn't. You wouldn't believe how long it takes to get anything done. It's disgusting."

He sighed.

"But don't let me get started on that. I would rather talk about you and this weekend. My flight gets in around one pm to-morrow; however, I have a couple of business meetings to attend. How about I pick you up around seven. We can check out that res-taurant. Does that work for you?"

They talked a few minutes more and said goodnight.

Nic was looking forward to seeing Jake again, however, she was glad he wasn't going to be there until the evening. That gave her time to check out her new plan.

The next morning, she was at the pet store. She had made a deal to walk one of the dogs whenever she had time. Nic presented herself as a lonely widow that needed something to do just to pass the time. She hated the words, just to pass the time, but that did the trick. Also, the fact that she posted a pretty hefty bond just in case something happened to one of their dogs while in her care didn't hurt.

She had been practicing how to slip into what she laughingly called her spy wear. She hailed a cab that allowed dogs, directing him to her planned location. Quickly she pulled out her wig out of her purse and placed it on her head. Took a fast peak of her reflection in her mirror, adjusted it with her one free hand, then pulled glasses out of her purse.

She paid the cab driver and slipped the lease around her hand a couple of times to get a more secure hold.

"Well, here we go Mr. Mooney. We are going on a nice long walk. I promise I won't let anything happen to you."

She felt guilty for switching dogs because she didn't want anything to happen to Tank, but not enough to not do it.

She had been going to police headquarters several times with the express purpose of finding out as much as she could about target locations. What areas in Manhattan that would likely have possible organization that would be dealing with human trafficking or harming Americans? She decided to take one section at a time. Lower Manhattan was her first target.

She had overheard some of the guys on the task force talking about an area close to Brooklyn Bridge near South Street Seaport. She spent hours researching the area. She walked Mr. Mooney up Dover to the entrance of Fish Bridge Park. Nic spotted a group of men that caught her interest. She tightened the reins on Mr. Mooney mostly out of nervousness. Slowly she meandered over in where the men gathered.

She tensed when she thought she heard a word on the target list. Mr. Mooney must have felt it, for he growled and began barking. At that moment a cute little miniature Yorkie sped up as close as his leash would allow him and began barking at Mr. Mooney. It was all too much for her canine companion. He took off toward the little pup. The sudden move caught Nic by surprise causing her to lose her balance. She caught herself but Mr. Mooney's fifty pounds was too much for her. He dragged her behind him. She had secured the leash around her wrist and couldn't let go.

Fortunately, the Yorkie owner scooped him up and took off in the opposite direction. Unfortunately, Mr. Mooney did not stop. He took off across the green lawn, almost slamming into the group of men she had targeted. Her wig was shoved to the side of her head. Her sunglasses crashed into her nose. All eyes were on her and the runway dog. She held on for dear life, trying to make him stop. She scraped her arm on a tree and hit her foot on a large rock.

Suddenly a strong hand grabbed the dog literally picking the fifty pounders up, bringing the big fellow to an abrupt halt. She plunged into the man's leg almost knocking him down.

"Oh my god, I am so sorry. Are you all right?"
He didn't say a word but pulled her up and headed toward the park entrance, with the huge dog in hand. Since her wrist was still attacked to the leash, she had no choice but to race behind him.

Before she realized what was going on, the man opened the door of a waiting taxi and had the dog inside. At the same time, he pulled out a knife. She started to scream, but nothing came out. The man reached around and cut the leash from her wrist. He held the door open and shoved her inside.
Before she could say a word, the cab door was slammed shut and the man disappeared.
Just as she opened her mouth to protest, the drive said.

"Where to ma'am?"

Chapter 9

Nicole was so relieved the man hadn't killed her, she forgot to protest, she simply told the cab driver the pet store address.

The driver waited for her, while she returned Mr. Mooney. She said her goodbyes, knowing full-well she would never return. While the cabbie drove her home, she canceled her credit card on file at the pet shop. She would call tomorrow and make some excuse, or not.

Once inside her apartments she limped into her bedroom and peeled off her clothes, then wrapped them in a plastic bag and tossed it into the trash, wig and all.

She hurt all over. Her left arm and both legs were scraped, her right wrist was badly bruised from where she had wrapped the lease around it, her foot hurt from slamming into that rock.

What made her think wrapping that damn leash around her wrist was a good idea? Who in the hell was that big man that rescued her? What the shit?

Slowly, she made her way to the shower. The hot water spraying down her body helped. What a disaster that was?

Once cleaned, dried, and clothed, Nicole walked into the kitchen, poured a large glass of wine, and down it. She crawled into bed and was asleep within minutes. By some mercy, she woke up around 6:30 pm.

It took her a few moments to realize where she was and what was going on.

"Oh God."

Quickly, she threw on some clothes and began putting on make-up. Each time she raised her arms it hurt. Everything hurt. There would be no sex tonight, she couldn't handle that. She couldn't handle the date either. She removed her clothes, got back in bed, picked up her cell and dial Jake.

"Hi you."

"Jake, do you mind if we postpone tonight? I am not feeling so well. Got a migraine, don't know where it came from."

"Oh baby, I'm sorry."

She could hear the disappointment in his voice. She felt bad.

"I'm in bed now. Just woke up. I am sorry, I was so looking forward to tonight."

"Sure baby, of course. Do you need anything? I can bring it over."

"I'm really sorry, don't be mad."

"I am not mad, just concerned. Why would you think I would be mad?"

"I don't know, you came all the way to New York, and I'm bailing on you."

"Your health is far more important than some dinner, or anything else. Look, I am here if you need me tonight. I mean that, anytime, anything, and if you feel like it tomorrow, I can pick up bagels. Just give me a call when you wake up."

"I will."

She hung up and rolled over and fell back asleep.

Damn, not how he imagined the night would unfold. He wanted to be with her, take care of her. Hell, he wanted her. Jake canceled the restaurant reservation with the promise to reschedule. Made himself a drink and ordered room service. He was listening to the news on TV, when the phone rang. It was the security group he hired to watch over Nicole. He couldn't believe his ears when his man recalled what happened that afternoon in the park.

What the fuck! He could feel his blood pressure spike.

"From now on, call me immediately, do not wait."

He was so angry he slammed the phone down.

"Migraine my ass!"

He had to do something fast to stop her. It was beyond crazy and it had to end. Yet, no matter what scenario he ran in his mind, it wouldn't work. Oh, he could shut it down, that was the easy part, but at what cost? He wanted her, he wanted her happy, and wanting him. Finally, he gave up and went to bed. Too many glasses of wine filled his body.

Troubled sleep was interrupted by the morning ring of his phone.

"Hello Jake."

His groggy voice answered.

"Hi you."

"Oh, did I wake you?"

"No, I am awake. How are you feeling?"

"Much better, I am sorry about last night."

There was a pause, then she continued.

"You know we had talked about going to the 911 memorial last time you were here; would you like to go today?"

"Sure, just give me some time to make arrangements. Glad you are feeling better."

There was another long pause between the two of them. It was as if neither of them wanted to lie anymore, so they remained silent.

Finally, Jake said,

"I will call you back shortly."

"Okay and Jake I'm really glad you are here."

The softness in her voice took him by surprise.

"Me too."

A few hours later he arrived at her apartment with a bag of hot bagels and cold smoothies. He had no idea what he was going to say to her. Mr. Control Freak had no control. When she opened the door he simply sighed and said.

"Hi you."

She stepped aside for him to enter, then gave him a long hug. He moved away to place the food on her kitchen counter, then turned toward her. They both just stared at each other, neither able to move. Suddenly, they were on each other, tearing at their clothes. This was crazy, she had to be sore from yesterday's fiasco. He should care but didn't, he wanted her more. It was crazy.

They moved to her bedroom. He pulled at her sweater, she ripped at his shirt. Finally, their clothes were on the floor. She pulled him to her. He saw her wince, and for the first few seconds, his thoughts went to serves her right, then immediately to wanting her safe. He saw the bruises, but it didn't matter. It was all consuming.

When the breathing slowed, he slid off her, but quickly encircled her into his arms, bringing her close to him. He cradled her, gently rubbing her arm as she placed her hand on his chest. Without looking, he knew she was asleep. He smiled, and just laid there. He felt a completeness he had never known. He slept.

An hour or so later he turned and reached for her, but she was gone. Jake rolled on the pillow trying to clear his head. He glanced at his watch. It was noon, they still had a couple of hours before they were scheduled to go to the memorial.

But for now, he was in the bed of the one woman he had always wanted but thought he would never have. She was everything he had ever dreamed of and more, all for the twist of fate.

She had awakened him.

When he finally got free of his ex-wife, he pretty much had his pick of whomever he wanted. Being a Senator didn't hurt. He wasn't rock star status, but close. The notches on his belt, so to speak, were many, but nothing ever lasted, they couldn't.

Over the past several months or so, he had begun to lose interest. He assumed it was his age, but this woman… this woman bought it all back and then some. He knew he was in way over his head. He knew she could make him the happiest man on earth or tear his heart to pieces.

Finally, he got dressed and walked into the kitchen.

"Oh good, you are up. I couldn't wait, I've already had one. I think you are right; these bagels are truly the best."
She handed him the plate and took another one for herself.

"Where did you say you get these?"

"R and D. It is located not too far from here. I pick them up every time I come to New York. I have been buying these for years."

"Do you still want to go to the memorial?"

"Yes."

"How about tonight? Do you want to try out that restaurant I was telling you about?"

"Yes, I would like that."
He smiled.

"I like it when you say that."

As they walked silently around the pool of names, it brought him to the fact that our nation had been attacked. Of course, being on the Homeland Security Committee brought it home to him every day. Daily briefings were passed to him first thing in the mornings but being at the place where so many citizens lost their lives, was almost overwhelming, even after all these years.

He had been here for the opening ceremony but didn't stay for the tour. He, like most of the Senators were there just for the ceremony, for the press. This time he really looked, really felt, and it was immense.

He decided they shouldn't go into the museum. Too many people were noticing him. This was still too raw, too emotional for Americans, even today. And it was political. Having been a Senator for fifteen years, afforded him a sixth sense about crowds. If they stayed much longer, people might start to gather around them. He didn't want to take a chance on it becoming ugly. He guided them toward the exit. Nic didn't seem to notice. She was drained.

"I had no idea it would be such an emotional experience. Thank you so much for arranging this. Ever since I moved here, I have wanted to go, but just didn't want to go by myself. Madison is just not ready. I understand, New York is her home."
Jake just looked at her.

"Nic, New York is your home now."
She looked back at him for a moment.

"Oh, I hadn't thought of it like that. I guess I still think of myself as a Memphian."

"Are you planning to move back?"

"She paused for a moment thinking about it, then laughed softly."

"I'm actually beginning to like living here. I especially love being close to Madison yet, I can't imagine myself not living in Memphis. It is all kind of crazy."

She thought for another moment.

"Plus, if they decide to have kids, I am where I want to be."

She sighed and changed the subject.

"Wow, I am spent. I know we didn't even get to the museum. Maybe we can do that another day. I am glad we have time to take it easy before going to dinner."

She closed her eyes for a moment.

"Did you say the name of the restaurant was Catch?"

"Yes, it is supposed to be one of the best new restaurants in the city."

Jake looked at her. She looked tired.

"I need to take care of some business, so why don't I drop you off. Our reservation isn't until nine."

Nicole smiled and leaned her head on his shoulder. They didn't hear the clicks of an iPhone aimed at them, as they entered the car. They both were silent most of the way to her apartment.

"Are you going to get a chance to see your godchild while you are here this time?"

"I would love that, maybe I could take everyone to lunch tomorrow. Do you mind calling her and see if that would work?" He smiled.

"Ask her is there is a special place she would like to go. Tell her there are perks being a Senator. I usually can get into just about any place, any time."

The car stopped in front of her apartment building. He walked her to the entrance. They lingered for a short moment, then he placed a quick kiss on her inviting lips. Suddenly he was on fire. He couldn't get enough. Jakes's hands grabbed the back of her hair to pull her even closer. He was lost in hot passion.
Finally, Nic pulled back. She smiled and whispered.

"Remember that when we get back tonight."
He pulled away, and kissed her fingers, then returned to the car.

"Man, I am drowning."
Across the street another iPhone had been aimed in their direction. Several clicks of the camera had been made.

From the Brooklyn Bridge to a seedier park of town, the group of boys once again were gathered in a dingy basement that housed a computer room. There was always an atmosphere of pressure to perform during their shifts, but today, it seemed to be a greater since of urgency.

Tempers flared as the instructors stalked the boys, yelling for them to come up with something new. Something that would help their cause.

"Twice now our operations have been foiled. Our trucks, guns, and our merchandise have been seized, and yet, you boys can't seem to find anything. What good are you if you can't use your skills to uncover who is doing this?" The man in charge picked up a ruler and slammed it hard into one of the boys, knocking him off his chair. Blood spurted from his ear. The boy wanted to scream but knew it would only invite more pain. He had witnessed this before over the past year only this time, he was the target. He stumbled back into his chair and began his search again.

A few years ago, he and the other boys were picked from their communities. The families were so happy and proud their boys had been chosen for this special opportunity. The families were told the boys would go to special schools from around the world to learn at a higher level. It was supposed to be an honor, but little did they know what special hell these boys were subjected to once they were taken. This group of boys' special hell was Brooklyn, New York, in the good old U. S of A. America, the place were dreams are supposed to come true, where they say the streets are paved of gold.

No one needed to tell these boys what could come next if they didn't produce something soon.

Quickly they typed as fast as they could trying to find something, anything, all the while, praying for the time to be up so they could escape. Finally, the buzzer rang. It was other boys turn to take their place in hell. Quietly, the boys climbed into a waiting van for their ride to the student housing, where they lived.

Chapter 10

Nicole slipped into something comfortable, laid on the couch, and dozed off. After about an hour, she woke with a start. What was the matter with her? She had completely forgotten about the words she had overheard from yesterday's disastrous park adventure. She gathered her convert laptop and opened it.

"Okay Miss Verdi, let's see if I am right?"

Moments later, she was searching the Homeland target list.

"Well, well, look at you."

She found two words that were on the list. She filled out her forms and emailed them to Mr. Thomas and closed Miss Verdi. She poured herself a glass of champagne and sipped slowly while she thought about their day. Being with Jake this morning was unbelievably amazing. Way more than she could deal with. It was supposed to be just sex, but it was becoming so much more.

Winn was supposed to be her one and only.

"Winn, I am so sorry, please don't hate me."

Nicole jumped at the sound of the land line. She listened for a moment then glanced at her watch.

"Yes, I can be there shortly, however, I have some plans this evening. If you could have the papers ready to sign when I get there, that would be great. Okay, I will be at your office in thirty minutes."

Nic quickly threw on warm clothes and hailed a cab. She spoke with her brother Jim while on her way to the attorney's office. Arrangements were almost complete to make Jim a full partner of Winn Enterprises, however, until that happened, she was the one to sign the contracts. This one was with the NFL. It was huge and had to be signed right away. Jim had been working closely with the NFL, and the New York and Memphis attorney's for months. All parties were on board. It was just a matter of her signature to make it official. Her speed-reading abilities helped her go through the contract quickly. Everything was as Jim said it would be, so she signed and thanked the attorneys for all their hard work and left.

As the elevator descended to the lobby, she realized some of the same boys as before were in the elevator with her, however, they were not the same. Instead of the cocky happy guys of times before, they didn't say a word. Their heads were bowed. They looked scared. Something was not right. She wanted to say something to them but didn't.

Back in her apartment, she took her time getting dressed, making a real effort to look good. Even though she was forty-eight, she was a beautiful woman that didn't have to try, yet when she did, she was stunning.

She opened the door for Jake, and he just stood there.

"Damn, woman."

She laughed and handed him her coat, then they headed to the car.

The Catch restaurant was such a magnificent place. All the reviews she had googled earlier were glowing, but even they hadn't done it justice.

She reached out to place her hand on his.

"I think I am in heaven; this salmon is beyond delicious."
He laughed as he rubbed his thumb over her fingers. Suddenly, he realized someone was snapping pictures. Quickly he removed his hand.

"I think we have just been outed, maybe we should leave?"
She just looked at him a moment.

"Well, too bad, because I am not leaving this fabulous food. Besides we are just two longtime friends having a meal together. What's the harm in that?"

Jake knew in his heart what was about to happen. He would talk to her later, but for now, he just wanted to enjoy this night with her sitting across from him. After dinner, they went back to her apartment, back to her bed. He knew better. He knew what could happen, yet when she asked him to stay, he did. Good judgement went out the window when she moved the way she did. Damn, it felt good.

Without looking, He knew she was asleep. He was in trouble. For thirty years, he had his feelings under control, locked down tight. As sad as it might be, he had become comfortable with the familiar sadness. It was something he could handle. Now that he had a taste of her, there was no going back for him. And yet, he had no idea how she felt.

He was beginning to know how some of the women he had dated in the past must have felt. They had wanted a commitment from him, something he could not give, ironically, because of this woman.

"Okay, enough of your pity party, you are a U. S. Senator for shit shakes. You are a very wealthy man, whatever you want, you go after and get. Why the hell are you being such a wimp?" With new resolve, he began to think of a plan of attack. He would have this woman.

Then he just laughed at himself, who was he kidding, he loved this woman, always had, always will. He would either be the happiest guy on earth, or his heart would be crushed beyond repair. Either way, he was all in. He pulled her closer and slept. Just before dawn he was met with a buzz of his cell. He looked at caller ID and frowned, then eased out of her bed and into the guest bedroom. He sighed and answered the phone.

"Yes?"

"Senator, this is Sargent Pennington from Police Headquarters. The Commissioner needs you ASAP."

"What?"

"Sir, I am downstairs waiting."

"Downstairs?"

152

"Yes sir, in Mrs. Robert's lobby."

He showered quickly, trying to clear his head. He had to think. How did the police know he was here? More importantly, why did they know? Whatever was going on, he didn't like it. As he stepped off the elevator, a man who identified himself as Sargent Pennington handed him an oversized hoody and sunglasses.

"Put these on, Senator, we are going out the back."

"What the hell?"

An unmarked car pulled up to the back door. The Senator was basically shoved inside. The Sargent didn't answer his query. Jake certainly was not accustomed to this kind of treatment. He would deal that later. Mr. Thomas met them at the back entrance of One Police Plaza.

"Morning Senator, follow me please."

He was led into a smaller room right off the conference room. The Commissioner was there.

"Jake, sit down please."

"Frank, what's going on?"

The Sargent left the room just as the Commissioner placed a folder on the table in front of Jake.

"Friday around noon, a woman we have now confirmed to be Mrs. Roberts entered Fish Bridge Park. She was with a rather large dog. After about fifteen minutes, the dog began to chase another dog, dragging Mrs. Roberts. Caused quite a spectacle.

Fortunately, someone came along and helped her into a cab. As we well know, this is the age of the iPhone, cameras everywhere. The dog dragging incident went viral."

"I know about that; it was my man that rescued Nicole." The Commission held up his hand.

"She had good instincts, since that is the location of an on-going operation. She sent an email detailing some target words she overheard. Once again, she was spot on, and the fact that she was in disguise was good, so that by itself is not an issue." The Commissioner paced around the small room.

"We have spent many months gathering intel on this group, we have a man undercover. This has been a well-planned, very detailed operations. It must be to ensure our guy's safety. What Mrs. Roberts gave us on her report was very important. She helped put the final pieces together. However, the fact that she dropped herself into an on-going operation is the issue. Still, we could have dealt with that. But this morning, we find ourselves having to race against time. We are having to scramble. The raid has to take place with-in the next hour, and that, Senator is the issue." Frank tossed the folder toward Jake. Confused, Jake opened it.

Inside the folder was a stack of photographs. The first several pictures were of Nicole being dragged by the big dog. The YouTube caption underneath one of the shots called her a crazy lady. Another related to the fact that she was going to be sorry she wrapped the leash around her wrist. She will be black and blue by morning.

He continued looking through the stack and then he saw it.

"Holy Shit."

"That one is on Page Six this morning. There is no containment."

Jake just kept staring at the picture. It was a photo of the two of them engaged in a passionate kiss. Her bruised wrist could be seen wrapped around his neck.

The Commissioner continued.

"Fortunately, it is not a clear photo of the two of you. However, look at the other two. These were on social media this morning. We have contained it somewhat, but it is still out there."

Frank sat down in a chair.

"Hopefully this will be a non-issue, but we can't take that chance. These cells have expert techs working 24/7 looking for things such as this. Someone somewhere might connect the dots. Connect the physical similarities of Nicole to the lady in the park or remembered her presence in the other raids. Because of that possibility, we've had to move up our timetable."

The Commissioner paused and took a long look at his friend.

"Jake, you and I have been in this business a long time. Shit like this can destroy a man's career, not to mention put Nicole in harm's way. Why didn't you tell me you were involved with her?"

"Believe it or not, it just happened. It's complicated."
Frank raised his hand once again to stop Jake.

"We can hope no one will put it together but we can't take that chance. She is a tall elegant slender woman. She has a certain demeanor about her that no amount of disguise can change, and there are hackers who can connect the obscure dots. That is their job. We can't be too careful."
Frank walked briskly toward the door, then turned to Jake.

"The intel she had provided us over the past weeks has been invaluable, as well as the program she has put together, but she can no longer go off on her own like that. It is too dangerous for her and our people. You know that don't you?"

Jake nodded his head, but the Commissioner had already left the room.

Within minutes he was on his way back to her apartment. He breathed a huge sigh of relief when he saw she was still asleep. Thank goodness he had decided to take her house keys with him when he left earlier. He quietly shut her bedroom door and went into the living room. He glanced at his watch. Only seven am. He had calls to make, things to set up.
Around eight, she came into the living room.

"Hi you."

She smiled and stretched.

"You are up and at 'em early this morning… and looking so serious. Is our government in crisis?"

"Morning."

He took in all her beauty. She was so cute with her hair rumbled and sleep still in her eyes. He just wanted to grab her and hold on forever, instead he said.

"John brought us some bagels, want one?"

She looked at him for a moment.

"I will get it; do you want anything?"

"No, I'm fine."

With a Diet Pepsi and bagel in hand, she returned to the living room. She sat down beside him on the couch.

He noticed she winced when she sat. He could see the bruises on her wrist.

"What is going on?"

"Well, we have kind of gotten ourselves into a situation."

He placed the photos in front of her.

"These were taken yesterday. This one made Page Six and these were posted on the internet."

Jake watched as she glazed at each photo.

"Well, we did discuss this. The only issue I see is we need to speak with Madison this morning, so she won't be blindsided. Other than that…"

She threw up her hands.

She paused for a moment waiting for him to agree. But he didn't say anything. He was gathering his thoughts. Suddenly he saw anger in her eyes.

"Look if you think this is going to jam you up Senator, then not to worry, we can stop this right now."

She started to raise from the couch, but he caught her and pulled her back.

She was angry.

"Stop."

"Please, Nicole just listen."

"Not necessary Senator, we can just call this a couple of rolls in the hay and go about our business."

She tried one more time to get up, but he held on harder.

"Let go of me."

"God Nic, don't you know I love you, damn it?"

He shocked himself for he didn't mean to say that. No way in hell did he mean to say that.

She eased back down and just looked at him.

Quickly he began again.

"I was called into Police Headquarters very early this morning."

He could tell he finally had her attention, so he took a deep breath and continued.

"Seems the Police and FBI have been conducting a convert operation in Fish Bridge Park for the past several months. Friday, when you showed up with that dog, they were working the area."

"How did they know? How did you ...?"

He ignored the questions.

"Pictures were posted on the internet of you being dragged by the large dog. Some remarks were made. Some people posted about the way you tied the leash around your wrist. They mentioned the bruises that are going to be on your wrist."

He picked up the one photo and placed it in her hand.

"Look again."

"This picture is on the internet this morning showing us holding hands across the table at Catch last night. The bruises on your wrist are very evident in these pictures. Some not so nice remarks are made suggesting I play rough. The Commissioner is concerned that the group they are investigating, or any other group might put two and two together. They might link you as the lady in the park as well as connect you to the other two raids. The Task Force moved up their timetable because of these photos. They have a man undercover. The operation is in progress as we speak."

"Oh god Jake, If I caused him harm, I would never forgive myself."

Jake could see the fear in her eyes. He knew how much she blamed herself for Winston's death, he didn't think she could take the guilt of another man's death.

"No, no, you have to understand, you have helped them. You helped them with the trigger words. The Commissioner will let us know when it is over. He said you were a huge help."

He kissed her hand.

"Now the other photo on page six shows us kissing on the front steps of this building. The Paparazzi knows your address and are already outside."

"Gees."

Before she could say anything.

"I don't give a damn about them. It's your bruises, we have to do something about them."

"Jake, you can't think anyone will actually believe you did this to me. Of course, I will set them straight."

"No, damn it, listen to me. Don't you get it? It is you. You! Very bad people could know where you live. If these people realize you are the one who has been collecting the intel for the police, you could be in real danger."

He turned to her and took her hand, looking at the bruises on her wrist. They were already black, blue, and green in color. Her wrist was swollen, and he knew it had to hurt.

"This may sound crazy, but we have to do whatever we can to hide the bruises. We need to be in public today."

By the look on her face, he could tell what he was saying was finally sinking in.

"Holy shit."

"I have made arrangements for a physician to meet us shortly. She will give you shots to numb your arm and wrist and deal with the swelling. With the shots, if anyone takes your arm or squeezes it, you won't feel the pain. Also, she will bring a high grade of medical make-up to cover your bruises. It will not come off all day unless it gets wet. The Doctor will be up shortly. She works with the FBI and will be incognito so no one will recognize her. John is bringing her here."

He stopped, took a moment, then began again.

"Now the most urgent issue is to talk to Madison. We don't want her and Zack to see these pictures before we get a chance to explain. Do you think they are up? Hopefully, they slept in, since it is Sunday."

"Yes, we need to call them now."

"Would you like for me to make the call?"

She nodded yes.

Madison answered right away.

"Hope I didn't wake you, but we need to tell you something. No, no she is fine. I am here with her now."

He took a deep breath and dove in.

"We just wanted to warn you that there are pictures on the Page Six and the internet of your mom and me. The pictures are cozy. We wanted you to know before you opened the Times. Being a Senator sometimes brings the Paparazzi around."

Another deep breath and he continued. This part he dreaded the most.

"Madison, there is a picture that appears to show bruises on your mom's wrist and arm. Some folks are making nasty remarks, suggesting that I put them there. I want you to know I did not. We wanted to tell you both today that we have started seeing each other, but these photos made us realize we needed to tell you this morning. We would like to come over in a few minutes if it is okay with you guys?"

"Yes, of course, can I talk to my mom?"

He handed the phone over.

"Hi sweetie, yes I am just fine. I am sorry about all this, but we will be over shortly, and we can talk more. Yes, sweetie, seriously, I am fine. Jake would never do anything to hurt me."

She listened to her daughter for a moment.

"Yes, sweetie, I promise. We will be there shortly, I love you."

After she hung up, she didn't say anything. She turned and walked to her bedroom and closed the door behind her. Shortly afterwards, the Doctor came. She gave Nicole the two shots. As Dr. Jones applied the make-up, she instructed Nicole on what to do and expect in the next several hours.

Soon they were in the car on their way to Madison's apartment.

"Mom, I have been so worried. What's this about your wrist, let me see?"

For the first time since she was born he felt the cold of his goddaughter's eyes. All these years he had taken her adoration for granted. But the morning light had brought him to her door as a man who was dating and per the New York Times, possible hurting her mother. This was a different Madison.

"Please sweetie, just let us explain."

Zack and Madison guided Nicole over to the couch, placing her between the two of them. A very protective stance not lost on him. He quickly took a seat opposite them and started to speak when Madison interrupted him.

"Mom, tell us exactly what happened."

"First let me say again, Jake did not hurt me, and secondly, we had planned to let you know today the we have started seeing each other. The tabloids just beat us to it."

"But Mom, those pictures on the internet show some definite bruising. Why would they do that? I don't understand."

Nicole took a deep breath and began, "I do have bruises; however, it is from dog walking."

Nicole winced. Damn, she wished she hadn't said that.

Madison immediately jumped in.

"Tank wouldn't..."

"Sweetie, of course he wouldn't, but you are going to have to let me explain."

Jake bit his tongue trying not to take over the conservation.

"I took a dog from one of the pet shops. I volunteered to be a dog walker. Let's just say it didn't work out. He was rather large, and when he started casing another dog, the leash was around my wrist and I couldn't let go. It was stupid of me to wrap that leash the way I did, but that is how I got the bruises."

Zack and Madison just looked at each other for a moment.

"Mom, you don't walk other dogs, you walk Tank. What is this all about?"

And then it clicked.

"OH MY GOD! That was you, you on the YouTube wasn't it? Yesterday the girls at the office were laughing about some "crazy lady" they were watching being dragged by a large dog. I walked by their stations and glanced at the video. I saw a woman dressed in some weird garb. Long blond hair. How could that...?"

Madison's voice suddenly got higher.

"Holy shit Mom, that was you in disguise, wasn't it?"
Her voice was cracking.

"You took another dog, so you wouldn't put Tank in danger.
You were out there again, weren't you?"
Madison whipped around and faced Jake.

"Damnit, Uncle Jake you promised you would put a stop to
this. You promised."
Jake tried to interrupt but Madison kept talking.

"Do you know how unbelievable crazy this is for my mother,
my nice southern mom... to be out there looking for terrorists. FOR
TERRORISTS FOR CHRIST SAKES! She is a housewife damnit,
not a trained FBI, or whatever it is called. How is this possible?
Why are the Police allowing this to happen? Are they behind this?"
Once again Jake tried to interrupt but Madison just waved him off.

"No, no I don't want to hear any excuses, you arranged for
her to have this job now stop it like you promised."
Madison whirred around and stalked to the kitchen. She had to get
some space.

Jake could feel Nicole's angry eyes on him.

"Your mom has provided some really good information for
the Police Department, so don't sell her short."
Madison was almost screaming as she raced from behind the kitchen
counter to face Jake again.

"Don't you dare go there? What? Are you trying to win points, so my mom will sleep with you? I wished my dad was here. This would not be happening."

She then turned to her mom.

"If dad were here!"

She stopped and swallowed hard, fighting back hysteria.

"Mom, you have to stop this, you have to."

Madison was talking ninety miles an hour saying whatever she could to make her mom stop.

They both were crying.

Zack stood closer to his wife, trying to comfort her, but she pushed him away.

Finally, Jake yelled.

"STOP!!"

Everyone turned to stare at him.

"We can straighten this out later, now we have to address another issue, a very important one."

Both Madison and Nicole started to protest, but Jake raised his hand.

"Nicole's safety."

They froze.

"It is a matter of the bruises. We need to publicly dispel the bruises rumor."

"Oh, I see what is going on, are you worried about your reputation, Senator?"

That hurt, but he had to keep talking.

"I was called into a meeting at Police Headquarters early this morning. There is a raid being conducted on a group that was in the park where your mom was yesterday."

"This is supposed to be for eyes only, but I am telling you, and letting you know it cannot be repeated under any circumstance. Frank thinks the chances of anything being connected back to your mom are very slim, but just as a cautionary measure he suggested we get photographed today showing no bruises."
The three sat back down on the couch and listened.

"I have made arrangements for Nicole and me to be photographed together. We will show there are no bruises on her wrist. We don't want to have any possible connection between Nicole and the raid happening now."
Jake looked at his watch.

"And to answer you about your mom doing any more of these adventures, the Police Commissioner has, in no uncertain terms, put a stop to them."
Jake could visibly see Nicole's anger.

"Maybe that didn't come out right"
He could tell she was beyond mad.

"But Uncle Jake, there are bruises, Mom just said so."
Nicole raised her arm and pushed up her sweater.

"Jake had Dr. Jones give me shots and covered the bruises so no one will be able to see."

The absurdity of it all hit Madison.

"God Mom, I wish now you had just stayed in Memphis. At least there you would be doing charity work and going out to lunch with your friends. Not chasing TERRORISTS!!! GOD!!! Dad is probably going nuts!"

Once again, she turned to face Jake.

"Uncle Jake, I almost hate you right now."

That one really hurt.

"Madison, you and your mom are the most important people in this world to me. Please know that."

"Well, then act like it and stop this madness."

Winston had told him about how strong his beautiful daughter was. How tough she could be on a person's heart. Jake was surely feeling it now.

"Well, since I am still in the room, let me say that I have no intentions of continuing with my adventures as you so patronizingly put it. So, let me just go out there in public and get this over with."

Nicole stood up to leave.

"Love you both. Will call you later."

"No, wait mom, we are going with you"

Nicole stopped in her tracks and turned to them.

"No, this is my mess, I will clean it up. You have to stay out of it. This will work so much better if I do it alone."

Jake jumped up.

"I said alone."

"Not a chance in hell."

He grabbed both of their coats, her arm and headed to the door. He turned to his goddaughter.

"Madison, I will call you later."

He shoved Nicole out the door before her daughter could say anything else.

Chapter 11

Quickly, they were in the back seat of the town car. In his most Senatorial authoritative voice, he said, "I will be with you."

She eased back on her seat as if to concede.

"Let me see your arm and wrist."

Not looking at him, she raised her sweater sleeve and let him look. He felt her arm, and looked at the make-up, making sure it was doing its job. Once satisfied, Jake made the call.

When he finished, he turned to Nicole.

"We are going to go shopping at an outdoor fresh food market. Just raise your arm casually to check the freshness of a fruit. The photographers will be waiting. Let them see your arm, discreetly of course."

He sheepishly continued.

"Also, you need to act like you don't hate my guts right now. We need to look like old friends, not someone involved in a homeland security situation."

"Well, Winston always said I was a good actor when I needed to be."

When the car stopped Jake grabbed her arm to keep her from escaping the confines of the car. He held her face and gently kissed her. He could feel her resolve melting for a moment, then she pulled back.

"Let's just get this over with."

Winston was right, if he didn't know better, he would have thought she didn't have a care in the world. They were just two friends having fun together. As planned, several well-placed people came up to them, shaking hands, taking selfies, and as hoped, other folks followed suit. Plenty of opportunities to show off her non-bruised arm and wrist.

Jake's photographers took shots of everyone within the perimeter. Hundreds of shots were discreetly taken before they returned to the car. Jake arranged to have John bring the pictures to Nicole's apartment. The moment the door of her home shut, she lit into him.

"You bastard, you lied to me from the get-go. Tell me, what you had to offer the Commissioner for him to agree to give me a spot of the task force? No wonder everyone there dismisses me. They all know."

She ripped her coat off and tossed it on one of the chairs in the living room.

"And why go to all the trouble. You already bribed the people at the U. N. to give me a position. Let's see in a matter of a few weeks, you have given me two pity jobs, a few pity dinners, and let's certainly not forget several turns of pity sex. My, my, wouldn't Winn be proud of the way his best friend stepped up. But that I love you part was way over the top don't you think, not necessary."

She bowed her head and repeated.

"Not necessary."

She stalked into the kitchen, grabbed a bottle of opened wine, and a glass.   Didn't offer him any.   It was only three o'clock in the afternoon, but she didn't care.

"Damnit Nicole, it is not like that."

She walked past him to her bedroom, slamming the door behind her. He heard the lock click.   In his fifty-two years, he had never experienced this kind of panic hurt.   He went into her kitchen, opened a new bottle and poured himself a large glass of wine, then returned to the living room.   Jake plopped down on the couch, and took a gulp of wine, as he stared out the window.   The grey sky matched his mood.   How did he let this get so screwed up? After a few minutes, he murmured to himself.

"Man, get your shit together."

Quickly, he began making calls setting up for tonight.   It might be over-kill, but he wasn't going to take a chance on anything happening to her.

When he finished, he punched in Madison's number.

"Did it go okay? How is mom?"

"She did just fine. She is in her bedroom now, and kinda mad at me."

Madison offered nothing.

"Sweetie, I would never, never do anything to hurt either of you. You've had to know that."

She sighed.

"I know Uncle Jake, I guess I got carried away earlier, but I am so scared. After you guys left, Zack and I talked. You were just trying to find something for her to do to get her out of her depression. As Zack said, who knew she would take it upon herself to go off on her own like that."

Madison paused to take a deep breath, then continued.

"That day when she told me about what she was doing, I saw a spark in her for the first time since dad died. She told me she had found a purpose, but she can't do that anymore, you know that don't you?"

"Yes, I know baby, she can't. The Commissioner did say she would have to stop. I think your mom knows it as well, but there are so many other important things she can do. Frank told me she had put together a very impressive paper concerning a language recognition program. Plus, your mom was very instrumental in stopping three very bad groups. Between you and me, that is pretty badass, and let's be honest, if it was anyone else, we would be cheering them on."

"Yes, but it's my mom."

"I know sweetie."

Jake took a deep breath and started to dive into the other subject, but heard Nicole coming out of her bedroom.

"Sweetie, I hear your mom. I will call you later."

As he hung up, he thought he heard Madison say good luck, but it could have been wishful thinking. He leaned back on the couch and looked at Nicole, waiting for her to make the first move. He saw a slight smile.

"Jake, I am sorry I said the things I did. I know you meant well, but you are treating me like I don't have a brain. Like the little woman. Throughout our entire married life, Winston never, never treated me like that, not even once."

Jake rubbed his face.

"God, I am so sorry."

He stopped, let out a deep breath and began again.

"Nic, when it comes to you…"

Nicole walked up, put her hand on his face, and kissed him.

He immediately responded, but she stepped back and just looked at him for a moment.

"Jake, I believe we are creating something special, but it is all too fast. I am nowhere near taking this to the next level. I am still too messed up. Sometimes I miss Winn so much I have a hard time breathing."

She took another step backward and continued.

"You are his best friend. My guilt of being with you is overwhelming. Whatever we are doing, we have to slow it down. Can we do that, for if we can't, I don't think I can continue? Right now, my foundation is too shaky. Am I making any sense?"

"Yes."

He smiled slightly and changed the subject.

"That shot is supposed to last twenty-four hours. We have some time left. Are you up for going out to dinner?"

She wasn't, but she didn't want to be alone with him all evening or be alone.

"Yes."

She gave him a weak smile and turned back toward her bedroom.

"Give me a few minutes."

He took a quick shower and was ready when she returned.

"Jake, would you make sure I have covered all the bruises?"

She handed him the tub of cover-up. Jake gently rubbed her wrist and arm making sure every inch was covered. Touching her, rubbing her felt so good, he didn't want to stop. Finally, she pulled her arm away.

"I think we should go, don't you?"

They settled in the back seat of the car.

"Look, we won't stay long, maybe an hour or so. Our people will get more photos. If other people take pictures, that will be an added bonus. Is the shot still working? Do you feel anything?"

"It's fine, don't feel a thing."

"And the other thing, we still need to act like we like each other."

Nicole placed her hand on his knee.

"I was a bit crazy earlier, sorry."

He smiled and covered her hand with his, then kissed her fingers.

Harry's Restaurant was always a good place to go. The food was excellent, as usual. People began to nod in recognition of the Senator. Pictures were taken. Things went well, until the server spilled a glass of wine on Nicole. He apologized profusely all the while trying to wipe the liquid from her hand and arm. It was as if he knew. Quickly, Jake stood up and grabbed the cloth from the man.

"Thanks, but it's not necessary, just the check please."

The man tried to take the wet cloth from him, but Jake held on for dear life.

He stared at the waiter.

"The check."

Jake grabbed Nicole's arm and steered her toward the back of the restaurant. He made a quick call to John.

"Have Matt stay in the front, while you pick us up at the back door. Drop us off and pick up the package of photos, then meet us back at her apartment."

Once back inside her home, she changed into more comfortable clothes and joined Jake on the couch.

"Now what?"

"John should be here shortly. He is bringing the photos taken today. We have to go over all of them."

"Don't you think this is beyond overboard."

"I know baby, but ever since 911, our guys look at every little thing. Way better to be super paranoid than the alternative. They just want to make sure there isn't any possible connection between you and the three events. Each time you were walking a dog. Even though you were in disguise the last time, with a different dog, you can't disguise your tall slender frame, your stature and elegance can't be totally disguised. Got a bit of good news; the YouTube video showing you and the dog have been erased."

"Can they do that?"

"Hate to tell you this but big brother is alive and well and can do just about anything it wants."
Jake chuckled.

"Of course, as a member of the Senate, I would have to lie about it."

"No offense, but we Americans feel you guys do that a lot."

"You have no idea how well and how often."

"All the time you have been Senator, this is just the second time I have heard you say anything negative about your job, and both times have been this week. Winn and I used to talk about you and your job. He used to worry about how you would survive being surrounded by what he perceived as a den of thieves. He called it corruption gone amuck."

"Did you ever worry about me?"

She laughed softly.

"To be honest, no I didn't."

He placed his hand on his heart as if she had wounded him.

"Well, I guess I asked for that."

Nicole didn't know how to respond, so she just placed her hand on his knee and smiled. He wanted to take her right then, but instead cleared his throat. At that moment, John tapped on the door. He gave Jake the photos, spoke with him a moment, then left.

"It's going to take us forever to get through these."

He picked up a pile and so did she.

One by one, they went through each photo.

They were told to separate them into piles of possible people of interest, one to five, with one being the most threatening. For over an hour they studied the faces in the photos and made their piles.

"Well, I don't know about you, but I am now officially crossed eyed."

He smiled.

"Me too, how about we stop. Do we have any wine, I would love a glass?"

"Yes, we do."

She went into the kitchen and came back with two large glassed filled with a Pinot Noir.

"I think you will like this. It is Redwood Creek Pinot Noir. It is quite inexpensive but very tasty."

She handed him his glass and he took a sip.

"Wow, this is good. I will have to remember the name."

"Okay, are we done yet?"

"Look, tell you what, let's go fast as we can through the rest. Let's treat them like playing cards, like Uno."

She laughed and they began. After a few minutes, Nicole put her hand out.

"Wait, wait, go back, Yes, that one, he looks familiar. I have seen him before."

"Where?"

"I don't know, the photo is not very clear, but I am pretty sure I have seen him somewhere. "

After a few more minutes they were finally finished. Jake picked up the photos and placed them back into the package placing rubber bands around the possible. He put them on top. He would call John in the morning to pick them up. John would make copies of the familiar ones and then drop them off at Police Headquarters.

She leaned her head back on the couch and closed her eyes, he followed suit. Jake found her hand and just held it. Soon they both slumbered. The sound of sirens from the street below woke him. Gently, he let go of her hand and eased off the couch.

He walked over to the window and peered into the night. A few young people were still wondering around. He glanced at his watch. It was three-forty am. He couldn't help but remember how many times he and Winston were like these kids, walking down the sidewalks of Knoxville, drunk, laughing, and completely oblivious of their surrounding and what could happen to them.

It made him sad to have first-hand knowledge of how evil the world could be. Being a ranking member of the Homeland Security Committee, he was privy to what horrors humans committed on each other, mostly using religion as the excuse. How God kept putting up with this was beyond Jake's understanding.

His thoughts went to his best friend who was gunned down, leaving the beautiful woman that was asleep on the couch, alone and messed up. Perhaps too messed up to ever truly be his. Suddenly, he felt a soft arm surround his waist. The most amazing feeling filled him, crowding out the darkness. Nothing was said. She offered her hand and led him back to the bedroom.

The next morning around 6 am, a buzz of his phone greeted him. The text read, "See Attached." He punched the app and waited. He was glad to see the pictures of their fresh market outing. No bruises showed, however, he was not so happy about the written words beneath the photos.

180

D. C.'s Romeo is back in town. The Senator from Tennessee has been visiting our fair city several times over the last few months. Perhaps, the stunning transplant from his state is the reason. Our tax dollars at work folks.

"Well, isn't that special."

She moved then turned over and went back to sleep. Jake eased out of bed, threw on his running gear, left her a note and closed the door behind him. He needed air, needed to think.

What he needed to do is fly back to Washington. Work was piling up, and he knew he hadn't been fully focused on his job lately. He was all too aware of the consequences.

Over the past fifteen years of being in the Senate, he had seen what happened to major players that lost their edge. It was open season on them. Early in his career he had participated in some of the arrows drawn. He was also aware that over the past few months his name had been added to the short list of people being considered for the next Presidential bid by his party's Super Pacs. Anything he did now would be under high scrutiny. The pictures of him and Nicole pointed the arrows in his direction, and anyone connected with him.

Every Senator worth their salt wanted a shot at the top spot whether they admitted it or not. He was no exception. He liked the idea of being President, but he hadn't thought much about how running for the job would impact his life, and those around him.

There was only six single Presidents and all but two were widowers. Only one divorced President. Americans expect a higher standard in every aspect of the life of their number one guy.

In the fifteen years as a single Senator he had always tried to be discreet. In this age of iPhones, smart phones, whatever you want to call them, anyone, anywhere, at any time could take a photo and have it uploaded in seconds. It was Senate 101. While there were pictures of him dating several different women, the only shots out there were showing him escorting ladies to a function of some kind. Always side by side shots, never anything indiscreet. Yet, when it counted the most, he let his guard down. When they kissed the way they did, in front of her apartment building, people snapping photos never entered his mind. He was too wrapped up in the pleasures, not protecting her, not protecting himself and their future.

Because of those few seconds, he had brought Paparazzi to her doorstep, and possible danger as well. And now what was he going to do, fly back to D. C. and leave it to her to deal with. He turned around and jogged back toward her apartment. He stopped short when he spotted the Paparazzi already setting up shop across the street from her apartment building. Damn, it was barely daylight. Jake ducked behind a building and made a call to John.

"Pick me up two blocks north from her apartment. Not sure the name of the street, just text me when you are on Bleaker, and I will find you."

He was glad he had written in his note asking her to call him when she woke up. Within an hour, he was in and out of his hotel and back to her apartment without being spotted. Once inside, he sat up his laptop in her living room and began his workday. Quickly, he sped through the hundred or so emails his assistant had tagged urgent, leaving instructions on what to do. He was about to take a break when his cell as well as his laptop lit up. Yellow lights were flashing and the numbers 729VOLS appeared across both instruments.

That was the code he and his assistant set up for the most urgent messages. It was their 911 so to speak.

According to Amanda, the story she had just told him was about to go viral in a matter of minutes. He had no choice, Madison was already at work, he couldn't let her be blindsided by this. He had to warn her. When he finished explaining what was about to happen, she didn't say a word, just hung up.

Jake leaned his head back against the couch and closed his eyes.

"Man, could this get anymore messed up."

Chapter 12

Jake sat stone still, eyes closed, trying to think. Moments later his cell buzzed, it was Zack.

"Is she asleep?"

"Yes."

"Good, don't wake her, I am on my way."

Shortly afterwards, there was a soft knock on the door. Zack didn't waste words.

"Madison called me right after you spoke with her. Senator, I know you have known this family a lot longer than I have, but you need to understand, this is my wife, my family now... my responsibility, mine. And I don't like what is happening. This has to stop."

Both men were tall, but Zack was an inch or so taller. He used his height advantage and leaned in.

"Madison and I aren't kids; we are well aware of what's been happening with Nic. We had a plan, yet without giving us the respect of a heads up, you came riding in on your white horse. Look, I know you meant well, but you have put their private lives out for public consumption. Man, what were you thinking?"

Zack didn't wait for an answer.

"You are a U. S. Senator for Christ Sake; I know you know better."

Jake started to respond, but Zack raised his hand.

"I am not finished. You need to make a public statement fixing this. I suggest you go home, and don't come back for a while. Do whatever you need to do to get the focus off my girls."
Zack paused for a second then added.

"My family."

The two men stared at one another for a moment, then Zack turned and walked to the living room, choosing to spread out on the couch, taking most of the space. Jake had no choice but to sit in the chair opposite him.

"People don't usually talk to me like that, well except maybe ...our... girls, but you are right, I have messed this up and I will fix it. Nicole and Madison mean everything to me. I wouldn't purposely hurt them, ever."

Once again Zack interrupted.

"Look, I know how you feel about them, about Nic, I have always known, in fact, Winn and I have talked about it."
Jake was struck dumb. The blood left his face. All he could do was stare at Zack.

"Quite frankly, I asked Winston, how come he let you keep coming around."
Zack could see his words hit strong, as he intended.

"It was after we had several drinks one night. I thought maybe he didn't see what was so obvious. He just smiled at me and said he knew you, trusted you. More importantly he trusted Nicole. He also said Nicole was oblivious to your feelings on the matter." Zack softened his voice a bit.

"He asked me to put myself in your shoes. What if I could never have Madison, ever?"

Both men sat in silence for a moment as Zack let his words sink in.

"You finally got what you wanted, but the operative word here is… what you wanted. It is so obvious what you guys are doing. Jake, you have been wanting this for over thirty years, but all Nic has been wanting is for her dead husband to come back to her. Just take a real look at her man, the guilt is eating her alive. And now you let that picture of the two of you get out. You, being a Senator, I would think you deal with this kind of thing all the time. How could you let this happen?"

Zack let out a deep sigh.

"I assume, this is political, right?"

"Yes, it seems I am on a short list to be considered for endorsements to run for President. I gave the opposition an opening and they took it."

"Man, I get it, but you get it too, right? You know what has to be done."

He stood up and headed for the door, Jake followed. Zack stopped and turned toward Jake. Once again, the younger man used his height. He stood close and gazed down.

186

"Time to step up, Senator."

He put his hand on Jake's shoulder for a short pat, then turned and walked out the door. Jake was used to dealing out the ultimatums, not being on the receiving end. Quite frankly, it stung, but as much as he hated it, Zack was right. It was time to step up. He started toward the bedroom, his mind still spinning from what Zack had said. My God, had he been that obvious? As he was about to reach for the doorknob, he heard soft sobs. Quietly, he entered her bedroom.

"Nic, are you all right?"

Quickly she began wiping her tears.

"Sorry, I thought maybe you had already gone."

It warms his heart to think she was missing him, but that thought was soon dispelled.

"I was talking with Winn, I do that sometimes, do you?"

"Yeah."

She patted the bed, inviting him to sit. Jake stood still, drew a deep breath, then started to tell her what was happening, but she began talking.

"I was just telling Winn about you, about us, actually asking for forgiveness. I have been doing that a lot lately. Ever since you came to town and turned my life upside down."

She laughed, he didn't.

"Jake, I never thought I would have sex with anyone but Winn, ever, let alone make love. That is kind of what we have been doing, no not kind of, it is what we are doing. We have been making love."

She looked at him with her big vulnerable eyes. He wanted to cry.

"Oh god, yes."

"I love it, and yet I feel so unbelievably guilty. I am betraying my husband with his best friend. What kind of monster am I?"

He wanted to go to her, wrap his arms around her, and never let go. She had just told him they were making love. It was the beginning of what he wanted, yet he knew what he was about to tell her would more than likely destroy this moment and maybe whatever chance he had with her.

He backed up a step and began.

"Nic, I probably told you how I feel too soon, but it is the truth, plain and simple. I do love you. I will always love you, and I too have felt the massive guilt just like you, but I think maybe it would be okay with Winn. Now that he is not here, I think he would be okay with it."

He gazed longingly into her eyes for a second, then looked away.

"I wish I could be with you right now."

He swallowed hard and began again.

"But there is something going on I need to tell you about."

He took one more deep breath.

"All of my years in politics, I have been so careful about having my picture taken. So many women out there…"
He stopped then started again.

"Anyway, I have always dodged that bullet, hell, I have been so good at it, several members of congress come to me for advice on how to maneuver the maze of cell phones and Paparazzi. Yet, all my expert knowledge goes out the window when it comes to you. I have become an idiot. I have been so wrapped up in you, I let my guard down. I let those pictures happen."
She smiled slightly.

"We discussed this already. While I wished they were not out there, I am not upset. It is no one's business."

"I wished that was the end of it, but it isn't, you see, there is a short list of names being considered to make a run in the next Presidential election. I have been told I am on the top of the list. What's happening is politics. Someone is using those photos to discredit me. It is all about politics. There is no other explanation."
He could see the look of bewilderment on her face.

"There is an article out this morning raising questions about how long we have been together. There are awful innuendoes about my involvement with Winston's death."

"Don't be ridiculous."

"Well, it's out there and more… more."

"I don't know if you are even aware of this, but back when Madison was christened, you guys asked me to be her Godparent. I set up a trust in her name, as a christening present."

"Well, of course I knew. I sent you a thank-you note, don't you remember?"

He just looked at her for a moment.

"Winn and I kept adding to the trust over the years. Since I was the finance person, I was the one who signed the papers concerning her trust but is was both Winn and me making the investment decisions. There is a paper trail of both of us signing papers on Madison's behalf. I just need to produce them when I get back to Washington. Winn and I held yearly meetings with Madison, ever since she was a teenager, to let her know what was happening to her trust. I don't know how much they have kept you informed. Madison's trust has grown considerably over the years. Today, it is worth several million. The thing is the media is making this into something it is not."

He took one more deep breath and let it out.

"Nic, they are accusing us of having a long-term affair, of Madison being my child. They are saying that is why there is such a large trust. Somehow they found out about it."

He could see her turn from a look of confusing to a mommy tiger in a matter of a second.

"Oh, good lord, this is completely crazy."

190

She flung the covers from her body and was off the bed, grabbing her clothes.

"Well, no matter how ridiculous it is we have to tell Madison right away, before she finds out another way."

She leaped for the phone and began to dial. He grabbed her arm to stop her.

The look in her eyes stopped him.

"I called Madison already, she was at work. I wanted to tell her before someone else did. Amanda said the story was about to be released."

"You talked to her before talking to me? Why would you do that? Why didn't you wake me?"

"I was just trying to...."

She waved him away.

"I have to talk to my daughter."

"We should talk about this... about what to do."

"No."

She took a couple of breaths to calm down.

"Jake, I need to talk with my daughter. You did not have anything to do with Winn's death, that is ridiculous, and as far as Madison goes, she is a grown woman. She knows perfectly well who her father is. Still, there is just too much of this Paparazzi and page six stuff. It has to stop."

He just stared at her then offered to get a car.

"The Paparazzi have already set up outside, but I will make arrangements to get you out of here."

"Okay, good."

"Nic, I will fix this."

But he could tell she wasn't listening. She had already turned toward the bathroom. He watched as she closed the door behind her. After John picked up Nicole, Jake called his office. Amanda didn't even wait for him.

"Senator, whatever you need."

"Thanks Amanda, first thing I need to do is get back to Washington. We need to set up a press conference. I am going to answer the bastards on this one."

He gave her a few more instructions on what he wanted done.

"And Amanda, make sure the plane expense comes from my personal account."

"Understood."

The moment he hung up with Amanda, his cell rang.

"Morning Jake, we would like to keep Nicole on the task force, but of course our hands are tied until you get this mess cleaned up."

Jake couldn't help but smile. The New York Police Commissioner was known for his no non-sense telephone approach. This morning he was true to form.

"Morning Frank, how did the raid go yesterday?"

"Mission accomplished."

The Commissioner cleared his throat.

"Just let me know when you get this cleared. And I trust this fiasco will not make a difference concerning our allocated Homeland Funds."

"Of course not."

"Good,"

The Commissioner hung up.

"Good talking with you."

He was still in Nicole's apartment. He showered, then went to work. John sent a decoy out front, while they slipped out the back, and into an awaiting car. Quickly they sped off toward LaGuardia, where a private jet awaited his arrival.

Before he boarded, he handed John a list of items he wanted taken care of, along with a very generous check of his extra service. Jake then offered John a full-time position as his New York Security Consultant and Logistic Coordinator. He gave him a substantial financial package. John just looked at him, as if to say, are you shitting me?

"I need someone I can trust to watch after Nicole and her family. Also, as a member of the Homeland Security Senate Committee, I need eyes and ears here in New York. Someone that is not politically connected. Over the years, I have used your services, I have come to know and trust you. I will take care of the financial end. You will be working for me personally. Your hire will have no connection to me being Senator."

He stopped for a moment and reached in his wallet for Amanda's business card.

"If you are interested, my assistant, Amanda will send you the contract. Look over it and get back with her if you have any questions. She is well versed."

He gave the card to John.

"If you accept my offer, I will want you to coordinate with the security team, I have in place here. I need your answer yesterday. It is that important to me."

John glanced at Amanda's card.

"Senator, you are a man I trust, so my answer is yes."

He chuckled and added.

"These zeros can't hurt either."

Both men smiled, then Jake turned serious.

"I want Nicole and Madison safe. Top priority, understood."

"Roger that."

As Jake's plane headed toward the nation's Capital, Yuri along with the other students were being bused to the school in Manhattan. While the other boys laughed and joked with each other during the hour-long ride, Yuri sat alone, totally emerged in his own thoughts. One of the boys tried to engage him.

"Hey, Yuri, what's wrong with you man? You used to be fun, now all you do is mope. Look, what happened to Pavel is horrible, but there was nothing you or any of us could have done. You have to move on man."

Yuri just stared at him then turned away and looked out the window. He thought to himself, you are wrong, I could have done something, I could have saved him, but I didn't. It is my fault he jumped.

The boy made a gesture then returned to his seat.

The guilt of not helping his friend was eating away at Yuri's soul. He had seen Pavel go down to the basement earlier that day, when his friend had not reappeared, he went down to the basement looking for him. That is when he saw Pavel tied up on that board. He saw what Adams was doing to him. He heard Pavel pleading for him to stop.

Yuri was frozen, he couldn't move, then Pavel turned his head and looked straight at Yuri. He will never ever forget those eyes begging him for help.

Instead he had panicked and ran when Pavel needed him most. He ran to the bushes and threw up. It took him a while to settle down, then he made up his mind to go back down in the basement and help Pavel. But it was too late, he had to get on the bus to go to work. In this world they lived in you did not miss your bus. You would be beaten with-in an inch of your life, so he climbed on to the bus. On the ride to work he decided when he returned from work, he would find Pavel and together they would figure out a way to stop Adams. Yet, that night, when he returned, he tried to find his friend. He looked for over an hour, with no results. Finally, he gave up and went to bed. Tomorrow he would find him.

However, the next morning one of his friends told him that Pavel had jumped from the University Building in Manhattan. If only he could have found him, if only he had not panicked, his friend would be alive. For weeks now, that's all he thought about. It was his fault that Pavel jumped. He had to do something. He had to make it right. He had to make Adams pay.

Finally, he came up with a plan that might work. First-of-all, he wanted Adams to pay dearly for what he had done to his friend. Secondly, he wanted the jackass to know he was the one dealing out the justice. However, he didn't want to get caught, so he had to be very smart about his revenge.

The bus stopped in front of the high-rise that housed their school in Manhattan. When he walked into the lobby, he looked for her as he had been doing for days. Finally, he saw her entering the elevator. He just made it as the door begin to close. When the elevator started the journey up, he turned to her.

He spoke Turkic to her.

"Good morning."

He made a point to look her directly in the eyes and smiled. To his relief she smiled and returned her greeting in Turkic. Then she said how sorry she was about his classmate's death. He got what he wanted. She responded to him in his native language. For now, that was enough. By early afternoon the Senator was in front of the Washington cameras.

"Over the years, I have made it a rule not to respond to gossip and innuendoes about my private life, however, in this case."
He leaned closer to the bank of mikes.

"My business partner, Winston Roberts, and his family have been dear friends of mine for over thirty years. They are some of the finest people anyone could ever have the privilege to know. His family and friends still mourn Winston's passing, and will for a long time to come."
Jake paused for a moment.

"When Winston and his wife asked me to be their daughter's godparent almost thirty years ago, I set up a trust for her as a christening gift. As time went by, her father and I managed the trust. It is a matter of record."

Jake picked up a document and waved it in front of the press.

"His signature is there along with mine. That article was a political move, period. I am sure you received a copy of the memo circulating this weekend. If you are any kind of journalist, you saw

197

my name on the list of people being considered for Presidential endorsements. While I had nothing to do with that list, my associates tell me the article published is an attempt to get my name removed from the list. This is dirty politics, pure and simple, and you are allowing yourselves to be used."

Jake made a point to look at the reporter whose paper printed the story, until the man bowed his head.

"Since, I have no intentions of running for President, this is a waste of valuable time. More importantly, someone tried to use my dear friend and his family. My attorneys have assured me they can and will pursue any and all avenues at their disposal on this matter. I trust this will not happen again. Be journalists, not gossip rags."

He paused.

"The press is one of the most valuable parts of our American democracy. Your job is huge. The country needs you. We need you to be there for us to keep us informed. The press is trusted to search for the truth. Don't abuse that trust, check your stories."
He paused once again.

"Check your stories or my attorneys will do what I pay them to do, and that is a promise."
He turned to look at all the press members.

"While I have no interest in running for President, I have great interest in protecting my friends, and I will stop at nothing that is legal and appropriate to protect them as well as the people of the state of Tennessee. Now for the only time ever, I will say… yes, I was in New York this past weekend, and yes, I am single, and I have a life. That is all that will ever be said about that by me or my staff. Now if you will excuse me, I have work to do."

The news media scrambled with more questions, while he and his security team walked to the waiting car.

As planned, several days later there was a picture of a beautiful lady with strikingly similar features as Nicole shopping at Bloomingdales. The words beneath the photo indicated that perhaps this was the woman the Senator had been dating for a few weeks. The article rumored that he flew to New York to be with her, not his partner's widow. The young lady played her part well. Again, as planned, a couple weeks later, there was another photo of the Senator escorting the same beautiful lady to a White House function.

Many weeks later, the young lady moved to LA where she was offered a role in one of the upcoming summer blockbusters. Things were getting back to normal, yet Jake had already tasted Nirvana and he couldn't go back. Christmas had come and gone. The world welcomed the new year, and the gloomy grey days of February covered the nation's capital. It matched his mood.

Nicole had gotten past her anger of him not talking with her first, before calling Madison. He was learning. He called her four or five times a week. Jake had John install a special secured phone in her home like the one he had. No one could trace their calls. She never called him, but she always answered his calls. Baby steps, but he wanted so much more.

He picked up the phone.

"Hi."

"Hi you."

"I have meetings in New York next week. I want to see you."

"I would love that, when will you be here?"

He wanted to say in a couple of hours, instead.

"Let me check with Amanda, I will send you my itinerary." There was silence between them, yet they both could feel the electric currents shooting through the wireless.

"There is a dinner I am supposed to attend, do you want to go?"

"Maybe not this time, I just don't want what happened last time to start again."

"Well, my takeaway from that is, there will be a next time." Nicole laughed softly.

"I am really looking forward to seeing you. I want you to see my new home, it has gone into escrow. There is a view of the Hudson. It is so much larger than where I am now. I love it."

"I don't know, your apartment will always have a special place in my heart."

They both leaned in.

"Let me get my schedule and I will call you back."

He hung up and immediately buzzed Amanda.

"I am going to New York, Friday, and I will need to be there the following week maybe ten days. Can you make the arrangements and adjust my appointments accordingly?"

Amanda chuckled.

"Well, it's about time."

"What?"

"I will take care of your itinerary right away."

"Good, call me as soon as you finish."

Jake fixed himself a drink and waited.

Finally, Amanda called.

"You are clear for Friday's departure. I have you on a private jet leaving around noon. You are booked in the Presidential suite at the Conrad. John will pick you up at your usual place. All your appointments have been moved to tomorrow or when you get back. I am emailing your itinerary now. "

"Thanks Amanda, I appreciate you."

"I know you do. Now go get your lady and get on with your life. You have been moping around way too long. Let's close this deal."

She hung up before he could say anything.

Jake laughed at himself. How could a grown ass man be so tongue-tied around a woman? The answer was easy. It was this woman.

She opened her apartment door to him. She smiled and so did he. They just hugged for a long moment.

"Would you like something to drink? I just opened a bottle of Champagne. Did you know there is a study just published, I think from Harvard, stating we should be drinking Champagne every day to ward off Alzheimer's. I for one am buying into this program. What do you think?"

He laughed.

She handed him a glass.

There was a second of two of awkwardness.

"Did you talk to Zack and Madison? Are they okay with me being here?"

She simply said yes and changed the subject as she turned to walk into the living room.

"You will have to excuse the boxes, moving day will be here before you know it."

She sat down in a chair opposite the couch and continued to talk about her new home.

"If you have time, I would love to show it to you."

"I will make myself available whenever, just let me know."

"Great, I will call the realtor and let her know. Jake this place is magnificent. I can't wait for you to see it."

She bowed her head and whispered.

"It is because of Winn I can do this. He left me very well off."

She shook her head as if to shake off the dark clouds.

"Anyway, maybe we can see it tomorrow, maybe noonish."

She rose from her seat and went into the kitchen. She brought the Champagne bottle back with her and refilled both their glasses.

He made a toast.

"To Winston."

They toasted and drank.

"Are you hungry, can I take you to dinner?"

"Do you mind if we just order in. I'm still a little gun shy. Don't want to start all that stuff again."

That suited him. All he wanted was to be with her.

"Frank said you are still working with the task force. How is that going?"

She went back into the kitchen and brought out a menu from Otto's.

"They have awesome Pizza."

She handed him the menu.

"Yes, I am still working with the Police. Just as a consultant, I only go in when I need to, and I only meet with Jason. I think it is for my safety. Actually, I like it that way. I work at home mostly. Right now, we are working on language programs."

She took another sip of Champagne.

"I have an idea that I ran by Jason, and he was impressed." She put down her glass.

"You see, I do have a special gift, but surely, I can't be the only one. There must be others just like me. So, we are trying to find kids that are born with special gifts. Right now, we are just concentrating on language and computer skills. We are taking it slow. We want to get this right. I plan to take this on an individual basis. Jason thinks it will be too costly to get government funding for small groups, and because we are talking about kids, there is an enormous amount of red tape. Say we find someone with certain gifts we then interview them and their parents. Much like the Principle did for me back when I was a kid. We will pattern an education for that individual child to fit his or her gifts, full of scholarships, the works. Jason says this kind of program will probably work better in the private sector. We are looking for foundations that might take us on. It is going to be hard to make it happen, but I am determined."

She picked up her glass again.

"Also, about once a month, I work with the United Nations. They were kind enough to give me another chance. Actually, I am a volunteer. I work with families coming into our country. Mostly refugees who have lost everything. It is horrifying what these families have gone through. The program I work with is designed to help make their transition a little easier. It is so rewarding."

As she continued telling him about her new endeavors, he couldn't help but see a different Nicole emerging. She was not the same woman that was married to his best friend. She certainly wasn't the depressed woman after Winston was killed. This Nicole seemed to have gone through the darkness and found her way to the other side. He loved her even more, but could she love him back? All he knew, he was all in, going for broke.

"Jake another program I am working on is called Words. A lady from our church back in Memphis introduced me to the program. Someone did a study on the kids of Memphis that fell behind in their reading skills. They wanted to know what happens to these kids. Well, as you might expect, it isn't pretty." Nic scooted closer to Jake.

"My friend found out that a child needs to have a fair comprehension of the thousand Day Words. This is the program named after Dr. Day, the person that came up with a list of the most used words in the English language. If a child doesn't get a gasp of most of these words by the end of the second grade, their chances of success in school decreases tremendously. Thus, the rate of potential dropouts is enormous. And this is the most alarming part, their chances of ending up in the prison systems goes up dramatically. It is critical that they know how to read. I am trying to start a program here in New York like the one in Memphis. Basically, we get volunteers to come to the school and spend an hour a week with a child. The goal is to help the children with their reading skills. I know it won't be easy, but it can be done. The Commissioner thinks it is a good idea. Now I just need to get with the right people to make things happen."

"I did not know this was happening in Memphis, in my state. I would love to know more."

While waiting for the pizza to be delivered, they talked more about words, language recognitions, and the United Nation programs.

After they enjoyed Otto's deliciousness, they headed to the kitchen to clean the plates. Once done, Nicole stared at Jake for a moment, then reached into the refrigerator for another bottle of Champagne. She picked up two clean glasses and smiled.

"Would you like to make love to me?"

He almost choked on his own breath, then reached for the bottle and glasses, and walked behind her to the bedroom.

It was beautiful, more beautiful, deeper, and more intense than all the times before. Their eyes locked on each other. As he began the physical joining of skin on skin, of plunging deep and pulling back, he truly found heaven. For the first time, he saw it in her eyes as well. He was home. They lay in each other's arms savoring the feeling. This time she didn't go to sleep immediately.

"You were right, what you said last time. I think Winn would be okay with this. I will love him forever, but I believe he would think this is good."

Jake pulled her closer and they slept.

Chapter 13

The following week was one of the best of his life, working on projects that interested him. The See Something Say Something program for Tennessee was coming along nicely. He engaged Congressman Conn to partner with him on the project. They particularly wanted to bring it to the schools.

In today's world children were being attacked in American schools. They need to know how to determine if someone is a threat or not. They discussed the fine line between keeping each other safe, and big brother stepping in.

Also, he started a program for gathering information on aged-out orphans. This was near and dear to his heart. There was so much to learn and do, but it was a start.

If it wasn't for Professor Edwards taking an interest in him, who knows where he would be today. He might very well be one of the ones who age-out onto the streets.

Another meeting he attended was about climate change. The meetings in New York were going in a positive direction. There were collective agreements with leaders across the world to join in. That was a huge step, however, the Senator had been in the business of politics too long to believe it was a done deal.

The country's governors were in New York this week. They were here to focus on the economy, all in all, a good week. Yet, the best part was coming home to her.

It had been an especially good week for Nicole. She settled in the back seat of Jake's limo he insisted she use. She had just finished a class with refugee families. The class was held at the U. N. She loved working with them. They needed so much and were so appreciative of anything they received.

The Commissioner had met with her and Jason earlier in the week. He wanted to know how the language recognition program was coming along. She could tell he was really listening, all in all, a good week.

Plus, Jake being in New York had been good too. They had spent many hours talking about their hopes for the projects they were working on. She couldn't help but think of the many hours she and Winn spent discussing their hopes and dreams. It should have been them spending this time together, all for the want of Chardonnay.

Nic shook her head hard, trying to shake any dark thoughts. Reality was, he was gone, and she had a huge hole in her heart, that would never completely be healed. Having Jake here helped fill the void. She laughed at herself. Who was she kidding, Jake had become so much more than that. After Winn died, she died too, at least parts of her. That part that allowed love, allowed desire. Winn was it for her. There shouldn't be any more. Then Jake, Winn's best friend of all people, comes to town awakening feelings. Feelings that she wanted to be dead, needed to be dead. The guilt had been overwhelming, yet not so much anymore, not so much.

Over the past weeks, her life had taken on so many new turns, yet parts of her wanted to go back to the darkness. After over a year, there was a certain familiarity in the loneliness. Her other parts liked the new self. The self that is now taking on important projects that could perhaps make a difference in people lives. Not to mention being on a task force of the NYPD. Things were crazy, times were scary, it was fun.

John dropped Nic off at her apartment. When she walked in the door, she saw Jake sitting in a chair reading the New York Post. There was a frown on his face.

"Hi you."

She took her coat off and placed it and her purse in the entry closet, then went over to him. After planting a kiss on top of his head, she asked.

"What's up?"

He handed her the paper. There were two new photographs. One of them walking on the sidewalk near her new home. The words underneath stated.

"Looks like the Romeo Senator and our Tennessee transfer are on again. Our sources tell us they are looking at apartments together."

The other photo was of her and Jake walking Tank in the park.

"Looks like our Tennessee love birds bought themselves a cute little puppy."

Jake didn't say a word, he just looked at her.

"I am not going to let this kind of idiocy bother me. I guess as long as you are a Senator, we will have to put up with this, but they need to keep my daughter out of it."

She smiled and added.

"I'm not too happy about my grand puppy being used either, oh, and let's add Zack to the list as well."

Jake took the paper from her and dropped it on the floor. He brought her forward onto his lap. They laughed and kissed. They were enjoying themselves just being together, talking, laughing, loving together.

Chapter 14

While Nicole and Jake were enjoying each other, an angry young student in New Jersey, lay awake staring at the clock on his dorm wall. Finally, the hands clicked together signaling the midnight hour. He slipped out of bed, threw on his clothes, and quietly made his way to the basement.

He was ready, he knew he was ready, yet he needed to take one more look just to double check, to make sure everything was in place. Tomorrow will be the day of reckoning. It will be the time of revenge for his friend. Adams would pay for what he had done to Pavel.

Yuri wanted to make sure the bastard would never be able to do it again to anyone else. He took inventory of all his weapons. Everything was in place for tomorrow. He felt sure he had thought of everything. All scenarios considered.

Just as he turned to leave, he felt something close to him. He twirled around, but it was too late. The baseball bat hit him across his back, causing Yuri to stumble. Another swing to this head, knocked him out.

It was almost impossible, but somehow Adams dragged Yuri across the floor and managed to lift him onto his special board. He used duct tape and rope to secure Yuri's muscular body. Once satisfied that the boy couldn't get free, he stepped back, and wiped the sweat from his brow.

"What the fuck?"

He tried to think.

Earlier when sleep wouldn't come, he decided to go down to his special room in the basement. Maybe there he could relax. He hadn't been able to sleep, since he had been beaten to a pulp. His mind went to a few days after Pavel jumped to his death.

That was when four huge men pulled him between two black SUVS, as he was walking to his car after work. They punched him several times in the face, gut, then three or four hard blows to his liver, kidneys, and private parts When they were through, one of the men leaned down near his bleeding head.

"The Boss said cut it out, or we will be back and cut it off."

Each man kicked him hard as they passed.

"Until next time, creep."

The four jumped into their SUVS and sped away, leaving him bleeding on the cold concrete. He couldn't move, partly from pain, mostly from fear.

Adams figured Pavel must have left a note when he jumped. He had been afraid of that, but when the police hadn't come for him, Adams assumed he was free. However, someone must have found something and passed it along to the boss. As he slowly walked to his car, it came to him that he had been given a second chance else wise he would be dead.

That was weeks ago, and he made sure he had been careful. He told the school that he had been in an accident, trying to explain the bruises, and limp. He hadn't been near the boys, mostly because it was taking so long to heal. His kidneys bled for days, and his liver took hard blows as well. Adams realized the men knew exactly where to punch for maximum damage.

Finally, he was beginning to feel better, and the old urges were back. He couldn't think straight, couldn't sleep. That's when he decided to go down to his special room. He thought maybe being in the room where things took place, might ease him.

He made up his mind he would take a video the next time, just in case he had to stop again. He would have to wait for a while, but he knew in his heart he would find another boy. Hearing someone in his special room was the last thing he expected. That was when he picked up the baseball bat leaning against the bookshelf. He didn't even remember placing it there. Adams swung as hard as he

could, knocking the man down, another swing and he was knocked out.

But it wasn't a man, it was a boy. He recognized him as he turned his limp body over. It was Pavel's friend Yuri.

"What the hell?"

Adams dragged Yuri's body to the board and somehow got him onto the board. He used ropes and duct tape to secure the boy. The adrenaline flow was beginning to wane. Adams body was shaking hard. He had to think. Finally, he checked Yuri's pulse. He was alive.

Adams ran his hands up and down the young man's body several times, then double checked the ropes and tapes. Adams left the room, double checking the lock. Thank goodness it was the weekend. That would give him time to think what to do. Quickly Adams made his way back to his apartment.

Chapter 15

The following day, in the basement computer room in Brooklyn, one young student sitting in the back of the room, raised his hand. The instructor walked to him.

"Sir, look at this picture in the New York Post."

The instructor glanced at the computer.

"So?"

"I think I recognize this woman."

"Well, isn't she a celebrity or something?"

"Sir, one day after our classes in Manhattan, Pavel, Yuri, and I were in the elevator heading to the lobby. We were talking in our own language so the lady on the elevator wouldn't understand what we were saying. We were just bull shitting, sorry sir, just messing around, having fun. Sir, this woman understood us. Before she got off the elevator, she spoke to us in our own language. She knew exactly what we were talking about."

Ivan was getting nervous; he knew the consequence if he was wrong. Just yesterday, one of his buddies got hit in the back when he said something wrong. Drawing attention to yourself was a danger.

His voice quivered as he continued.

"Sir, I… "

He bowed his head.

"Speak up boy."

"I think she might have been that woman on YouTube in the Fish Bridge park right before we were raided."

That got the instructor's attention.

"Talk to me."

"Well, sir this may be a stretch, but I think I may have found something."

His nerves were getting the best of him.

"But I could be wrong."

He wished he had kept his mouth shut.

The instructor needed a win. These boys hadn't come up with anything lately. His manager had been making innuendoes about his abilities to manage.

"Just tell me."

"When I saw this picture, I thought something about her looked familiar. She is tall, slender, and something about her, you know, rich."

He typed a few commands on his laptop and stopped.

"This is the woman at Fish Bridge Park, and this is the picture of Mrs. Roberts from page six. I placed one image on top of the other. You can see the similarities, same height, same arm length, and so on. Look the YouTube video of the big dog and the lady. Notice the placement of the lease around her wrist. Now look at the bruises found on this picture of her and the Senator. The videos and pictures of Mrs. Roberts and the lady at the park have been erased from the internet. Only people with my kind of skills can retrieve them. I think someone from the New York Police Headquarters erased them."

Once again, he typed a couple of commands, matching the bruises on her wrist.

"Sir, if you throw in the fact that the Senator is on the homeland security committee, things kind of add up."

Ivan wiped the sweat from his upper lip with his sleeve and continued.

"But she is an old lady. Why would Homeland hire someone her age for field work, that just doesn't make sense? I could be wrong sir."

"Make me a hard copy, and I will look it over."

Chapter 16

It was late morning and neither Jake nor Nicole had any appointments. They were enjoying just being together. Both were drinking their smoothies and nibbling on toasted bagels at her small dining table in the living room.

Jake put down his glass and looked at her.

"The other day, you said something about as long as I was Senator, the Paparazzi would be around. Well, there is something I want to talk to you about. What if I didn't want to be Senator anymore?"

She interrupted.

"Have you decided to run for President."

He just looked at her for a moment.

"How would you feel if I did?"

"That is your decision."

"What if it was yours as well?"

When she started to get out of her chair, he held up his hand to stop her.

"Just let me explain. Ever since that first time we were together, it changed me. I know that sounds cheesy, but just hear me out."

She eased back down and sipped her smoothie.

"You know my background; you know I was dropped off at a church doorstep when I was born. You know that I lived in foster homes and orphanages. You know that Professor Edwards and the game of football changed my life. Because of the two, I was able to have money and gain scholarships to UT, where I met Winn. He introduced me to his family, and they basically adopted me. Besides Professor Edwards, I didn't know family, I didn't know normal. But with the Roberts, I was around a good, loving, salt of the earth family. They made me want to be a better person, do better. Winn and his family are the reason I am where I am today. So, when he died, I lost my foothold."

Jake rubbed his forehead.

"I'm getting off track."

He stood up and faced her.

"What I am trying to say is because of Winn, his parents, and Professor Edwards, I was able to get my shit together, to become a stable human being. Because of Winn, I was able to gain enough courage to run for Senate. Being elected to the Senate has been a huge honor. I have worked long and hard to do my best for Tennessee, however lately I find I am on automatic pilot. I know what to do and I do it, and to be frank, I am very good at it. Thus, the party has expressed an interest in me as a possible candidate for President. They are pushing me for an answer."

He picked up his smoothie and began pacing.

"Ever since we were together, I have begun to open new doors in my mind. You have helped me to open them."

He smiled and put his smoothie down on the table again.

"Since I have been with you, I have begun to feel, not just do. I don't know if this makes sense. Look, I love that you are trying so hard to carve a meaningful place for yourself. Just in these few months, you have come so far. I love watching you find your passion. Do you know how your eyes light up when you talk about Words, and the determination in your voice when you speak of Human Trafficking issues, as well as the language programs you are working on."

Jake grabbed his smoothie one more time and took a large gulp.

"I told the committee; I would let them know my answer first of next week. But, quite frankly, the more I think about throwing my hat into the ring, the more I feel nothing but dread. I think maybe I am burned out. I am tired of making the "bridge to nowhere" deals just to get money for things like educational programs. I am tired of watching what I do get for my state, being parceled out to a friends and family program. Do you know funds for a police program that I worked my ass off to get for the state, has already been parceled out? The powers at be, of one of our largest cities allocated a hundred thousand dollars of that money to his girlfriend. When asked, he said it was for Public Relations. What a joke it is, and it happens all the time, all over the country. I hate it."

He stopped pacing.

"And speaking of hate, there is something happening in our country. The few people I have discussed this with are unwilling to entertain the notion, but I see it. There is a swelling of anger out there. I think it is mostly because of so many jobs going overseas, and I fault Congress for that."

He began to pace again.

"Congress is so wrapped up in defeating the other side, they don't see what is happening. Or they see and don't care. It's like a weekend football game. Got to win at all costs and to hell with the country, and nothing is getting done."

Jake took a breath.

"Plus, I think there is a backlash because our President is black. I am ashamed to admit that, but I see it out there, and it is growing, no matter how much he has accomplished, no matter how far we have come from the enormous economic disaster that was happening when he took office. I think whomever runs for our party is going to have a very hard time of it. The leaders of the party don't think so, but I do. And another thing, the party thinks the country is ready for a woman. We should be, but we are not. No, I think after a black man, if the party is going to have a chance to win, a white man is going to have to be the party's choice. I find that very disgusting and disturbing, and I hope I am wrong. Of course, I can't say any of these things to anyone else but you and Amanda."

222

Jake stopped pacing and sat down on the couch. She joined him.

"Congress is the place where big changes for the good of the country should take place, but it is not happening. It has become so partisan, so corrupt. I am a part of this body of government, and since there are no term limits, we can pretty much stay as long as we want, it's sad, but true. I fault the American voters for that. The polls state that congress has such low approval ratings, yet the people just keep voting the same people in. However, the Presidential race is where all the attention will be. All that anger and hate I see out there will be focused on that race. From what I am seeing out there, it is going to be a very ugly time for our country. I just don't have the desire to be a part of the process. I really don't. Someone is going to tap into all that anger and use it to get elected."

He took another drink.

"Plus, Homeland is looking into foreign governments using cyberspace to mess with our elections. We are looking into how that can happen. And trust me it is happening."

He paused for a moment.

"I am beginning to think the private sector is the only way to get the important social issues addressed. Things like climate change, education, equality for all citizens just to name a few. I have the money. I could get things done that I can't get done in the Senate. I have been very blessed, and I want to give back, I need to give back. I came from nothing, dropped on a church doorstep for Christ sakes. I am where I am today because I had people help me when I needed it most. I have to give back. I want to be that person that helps someone who has nothing.   I want to help them accomplish their dreams. Being with you has helped me to rethink my priories. I want to have passion again I want to have a purpose. Lord knows I have been overly blessed especially my financial endeavors. This is not a spur of the moment thing. I have been thinking about this for a while. I have been thinking about moving to New York."

He continued quickly before she could say anything.

"I am planning to find a home here. I have been talking with a number of people about starting a nonprofit foundation. My interests are climate change, and the security of our nation just to name a few."

He stopped and looked at her with a slight grin on his face.

"I am thinking maybe you might consider teaming up with me to run it. It would be a great place to build on your Words program and your human trafficking endeavors. Look, I have plenty of money, so do you. And this could be a good place where we could make a difference. We could have the freedom to put our time and talent to good use. And just maybe we could control how we get things done. You don't have to say anything now, just think about it."

"Can I ask you one question?"

He just looked at her.

"Would you quit the Senate before I get a chance to meet, The Boss, because that could be a deal breaker?"

He laughed, reached down and grabbed her off the couch. They laughed as he swung her around and round. He looked down at his watch.

"I hate to leave, but I have a meeting shortly. It shouldn't take too long; I will buzz you when I'm through."

"Sounds like a plan. I will walk out with you. I need to run by Duane Reade and pick up some supplies. I will meet you back here."

He watched as she crossed the street and entered the store. Jake smiled to himself as he got into the car and headed to his meeting.

Chapter 17

Yuri opened his eyes but couldn't see. He tried to move but couldn't. He was frozen with fear. He tried to think, but everything was a blur. Why couldn't he see, move? Finally, survival mode kicked in as his brain began to recall what had happened.

Something hit him hard enough to knock him out. He realized he couldn't move because he was bound, wasn't able to see because it was black dark. Adams must have come down to his hole. He must have knocked him out and tied him to the board he had Pavel on. Cold chills ran down his spine.

No way in hell was that going to happened to him, yet here he was, tied up, just like his friend had been.

He was beginning to panic. He screamed, trying to find purchase. He planned for every scenario of what could happen, but not this one. Panic fear blanketed him. Once again, he screamed. He began twisting back and forth, trying to get free. Suddenly, he remembered he had taped a knife underneath the board, just in case everything went to hell. Well, hell was here.

Countless tries later, a small ray of hope formed when he felt movement from his bounds. He bled from the friction of the rope around his wrist. After several more minutes, he felt it loosen some more. Thirty-or-so minutes later, he stretched his hand around and underneath the board to reach the knife. Over and over he tried, until finally he felt the blade. His bleeding fingers wrapped around the sharpness, cutting into his skin. The pain was unbearable, but he wanted freedom more.

Yuri almost lost his grip twice, still he held on enough to bring the knife around to his body. He twisted it to cut the tape, then the rope. Shear adrenaline kept him from giving into the pain. Finally, he was free. He removed the rest of the tape.

Quickly, he stood and stumbled to the floor. Slowly he regained himself and stood up. He reached for the light switch, and it almost blinded him. After several moments he scrambled to grab his backpack he had hidden. In it was a first aid kit. He had thought he would need it after he beat the shit out of Adams. It didn't work out that way, he needed it more.

Besides the first aid kit, he packed a change of clothes, gloves and a cap plus all the money he and Pavel had saved. Both the boys put aside almost every penny they made. After Pavel died, Yuri took his friend's money. They both dreamed of the day they would accumulate enough to go back home. Another plan shot to hell.

Yuri figured he didn't have much time to get out of the building before Adams came back. Fortunately, there was a sink in the room, so it didn't take long for him to clean up, bandage his wounds, and change clothes. He then climbed the stairs and limped out the door into the frozen night.

His whole body shook, for he knew there was no going back for him. He was good as dead, if he didn't make it to Manhattan.

Finally, he made it outside the student housing area. He began to breathe again as he walked to the bus station, he had scoped out days earlier.

He hurt all over. His hands, wrist, and head were still bleeding. He knew he would not be able to get on the bus if he was still bleeding. There would be too many questions, and he couldn't afford for the police to get involved. Above all else, he was an illegal in this country. Years back they found out the student visas were fake. That was the biggest hold the group had over the boys. Well, that and treason. Yuri slipped into the bus station's bathroom to clean his wounds. Once again, he was grateful for the first aid kit. The gauze and bandages covered his wrist and hands while his cap and hood covered his head.

He purchased a ticket with cash and waited. Finally, it was time to board the bus to Manhattan. He took a seat and held his breath until the bus headed to Manhattan. Finally, he let out a breath, and leaned his head against the window. The adrenaline slowed as exhaustion took over. He slept.

"Young man, time to wake up, end of the line."

"Thank you, sir."

Yuri ignored the bus driver's questioning look and made his was out onto the streets. He walked slowly toward the building that housed his school. Fortunately, there were a couple of benches as well as some landscaping just outside the building. It was not unusual for students to sit outside and study. He was glad he had tossed a paperback book in his backpack. He sat on the bench for what seemed hours waiting for her. Finally, he spotted her walking toward the building. Slowly he got up from the bench. He followed her into the building and watched as she entered the elevator. He knew where she was going. She usually spent about an hour with her attorney. He needed to catch her when she was leaving. He couldn't afford to be stopped and questioned. Yuri knew he was taking a huge risk depending on a total stranger, but he had no choice. He had to talk to her. He would wait for her even if it took forever. She was his only hope. Yuri went into the men's room to clean his wounds and replace his bandages. He stood in a corner to the lobby behind a large plant trying to make himself invisible, never taking his eyes off the elevators.

Nicole signed some more NFL papers her brother Jim had faxed to her attorney's office. She grabbed her package she had just purchased from Duane Reade, thanked Raymond and his staff, then left.

As she was riding the elevator down, she realized this was the first time she had left Raymond's office without tears. She smiled at the thought.

Once in the lobby she decided to go to the ladies' room before catching a cab. It was nice that the bathroom was empty. She took a moment and just stared at her reflection in the mirror. She stood as she watched a single tear drop from her eye and travel down her face, onto her coat.

Her thoughts went to Winn.

"Thank you so much for being in my life as long as you were. Thank you for your love, and for Madison."

Suddenly, someone burst into the bathroom.

Nicole turned and screamed.

"Holy, Crap, Shit."

The wild-eyed young man placed his finger to his lips for silence. In his native language, he pleaded.

"Please help me, they are going to kill me."

Nicole just stared at the boy, unable to speak, then it came to her, using his language she spoke to him.

"You are one of the boys in the elevator? You talked to me the other day."

"Yes, yes please help me. If they find me, they will kill me. I have information."

"Information?"

"Yes, for your government, for your homeland, but I can't go to the authorities. Please help me, help me."

"Why can't you?"

She paused for a moment, then said.

"Never mind, I think I understand."

Nicole reached in her purse and pulled out her cell to call Jake, then changed her mind. She made another call. As she waited for someone to answer she saw the shear panic on the young man's face.

She smiled and raised her finger as if to say just a moment.

"Hello, this is Nicole Roberts, is Raymond still there?"

"Yes, just a moment, please."

"Raymond, I need your help, I am on my way back to your office, I will explain when I get there."

She hung up before Raymond get a chance to ask any questions.

Nicole pulled some paper towels off the roller and handed them to Yuri.

"Here, clean your face. There's blood."

Once done, she grabbed the towels and threw them in the garbage.

"Stay close behind me."

Again, in Turkic, she asked.

"Do you speak English?"

"Yes."

"Good, what is your name?"

"Yuri."

Nicole scoped the lobby for anyone suspicious, like she would know. Quickly, they made a dash to the elevators. Once inside, she punched the nineteenth floor, all the while praying no one would enter the elevator. They were in luck for soon they were at the door of her attorney's office.

She noticed the frightened look on Yuri's face as he stared at the office across the way. She shoved him into Raymond's office. The big man stood with his mouth gaping open.

"What the f——?"

"Raymond, can we go into your office, we need your help."

Every instinct in him wanted to scream, hell no, but Winn Enterprise was his gold mine, whatever crazy this was, he knew he wouldn't say no. Nicole whispered.

"No one must know we are here."

Raymond told his assistant to hold all calls, then shuffled both Nicole and the wounded young man into his office and shut the door.

"Raymond, we need to help him."

She placed her hand on Yuri's shoulders to show her support.

"Tell Mr. Raymond your story. He is my attorney; he will know what to do."

Holy Crap was all Raymond could think of as he listened to Yuri. If the boy's story checks out, this could be huge.

"Okay, I have heard enough for now. Let's get you cleaned up and something to eat. Excuse me for a moment."

He left the room and Yuri just stared at Nicole. Neither said a word. Moments later, Raymond returned with one of his male assistants.

"Yuri, this is Mr. Tom Reed. He is going to escort you to the men's room. There is a shower in there. You can get cleaned up. Tom is going to get you clean clothes and something to eat. In the meantime, I will start the ball rolling on how to keep you safe and get your story to the right people."

Raymond looked at the scared young man.

"Do not worry, we will handle this. We will keep you safe." Before Yuri could say anything, Mr. Reed led him out of Raymond's office.

"Raymond, I know this is crazy stuff, but thanks for listening to him. Do you really think you can keep him safe?"

"We are sure as hell going to try, but first I need to call a doctor for him. He is pretty beat up, and his eyes appear to be dilated, he may have a concussion."

Once he finished the call to his doctor, he turned to Nicole.

"The doctor is on his way."

He pulled from his desk a legal pad and pen.

"If all this checks out, we need to get the Senator on board, he is Homeland Security. But I need to get the legal issues straight first. Don't say a word to the Senator or anyone else until I can get the legals in place, then I will call you."

As he wrote on the legal pad, he thought about what had just happened. If he played this right, it could mean great things for his firm.

"Is there anything else I can do for Yuri?"

"No, we can take it from here. I need to make sure we can clean up his immigration status first. We will keep him here as our guest."

"Okay then, I am headed home. But first I want to speak to Yuri. Raymond thanks again for helping us, for helping Yuri."

Once Yuri cleaned up, he sat down to eat, Nicole pulled up a chair opposite him. She explained to him that Mr. Raymond would work on getting his immigration status cleared up first. She told him everything would take time and he could trust Mr. Raymond to do the right thing. That he had to stay put until everything got straighten out. Nicole prayed that it could. Then she said she would see him in the morning. She got to the door and turned to smile at him. Nic saw the fear in his eyes.

She picked up her purse and left, as Raymond began the work to help Yuri. When she stepped out into the hallway, it hit her where she had seen that man at Madison's party. Mr. Billings was one of the men coming out of the University offices a few weeks back. He was probably connected to the awful things that were happening at the school. She would tell Jake about him when she got back home.

She walked out onto the street and raised her hand for a cab. As the cab turned onto Bleaker Street, Nicole realized she had left her purchases in the ladies' bathroom.

"Sir, you can let me off at Duane Reade."

She paid the fare and went into the store. She was glad it was a different lady at the register, so she didn't feel the need to explain her duplicate purchase.

However, as she gathered her purchase, and turned to leave, the same register lady as before came around the aisle and smiled at her. Nicole smiled back.

"Somehow, I lost my supplies I purchased earlier, so I am back for duplicates."

Once outside, she wrapped her scarf tighter and began her walk to her apartment. Nicole chastised herself.

"Really Nic you don't have to explain everything to everybody."

Chapter 18

Donald Billings hung up the phone and walked over to the bar in his office. He poured a drink and said to himself.

"I warned them, over and over, I warned them."
He picked up his phone and made a call.

"Pence, I need you to clean the University office tonight. Everything needs to be sterilized. I'll have further instructions for you. Call me on the secure line before you enter the building."
He was silent for a moment.

"Also, I have been informed the attorney's office across the hall will be in full use tonight. Make sure they are not disturbed. They are not to know you are there."

"Understood."

"Time of completion needs to be before dawn. And I need you to clean my offices. Everything must be removed."

"Yessir."

Billings finished his drink, then preceded to clear out the final papers from his office. Actually, he had been clearing the paperwork for the past week. This morning, he informed his beautiful young assistant, the office would be shut down for renovations. There was no reason to tell her they would not be back. As he handed her an envelope of cash, and her passport, he instructed her to leave for the airport immediately. There would be a private jet awaiting their arrival.

She was told her New York apartment would be looked after by his staff. Instead, Pence had already been instructed to clean and shut it down. She would not be going back there. He told her not to say a word to anyone. He implied they were going to check out a business acquisition. He had done this many times before, so, except for the suddenness, it wasn't anything that would concern her. Two men accompanied her to the plane carrying her luggage; however, their main job was to make sure she talked to no one.

For half a moment, he thought about having Pence get rid of her, but decided against it. She was beautiful, loyal, and she had no clue what was going on in this part of his business. Besides, he had spent too much money grooming her to just throw her away, at least, not yet.

Carrie James had worked for Mr. Billings over seven years. She had been treated very well. Exquisite housing, beautiful clothing, wonderful trips, fabulous dinners, and jewelry, in fact, she wanted for nothing.

Since she had no family left, Mr. Billings was as close to one she would ever have.

She had met him at the Miss America, Kansas Pageant when she was a senior. He was one of the judges. She didn't win, but she considered herself very blessed because she had made a friend in Mr. Billings. He had taken a special interest in her.

When her parents, grandmother, and younger brother were killed in a car crash just two weeks after she graduated Mr. Billings basically saved her life. She had no other family and had no idea what to do. She was frozen. However, when Mr. Billings heard about the tragedy, he flew from New York to her rescue. He took care of everything. After the funeral, he offered her a job. She would forever be grateful.

Even though she had entered his employment with a business degree from the University of Kansas he insisted she continue her education. He paid for it all.

Three years ago, she completed her PHD in Arts. She suspected the road to her Doctorate was smoothed by him. Mr. Billings hired a personal trainer to keep her in shape. At his insistence, she had attended finishing school, as well as several etiquette and diplomacy courses. She knew every fork on the tables, knew the protocols of most countries, and conducted herself impeccably.

He treated her more like his daughter, well, daughter-like, for there was a certain level of care but no fatherly feelings. Yet strangely, and thankfully there was no sexual favors required. She was so grateful to him it never occurred to her that he only wanted her for her beauty, and her elegance, not her intelligence.

Carrie was summa cum laude from the University of Kansas. She was fluent in three languages, top of her class in business finance as well as a computer genius. Her job was to answer his phones, coordinate his appointments, and do research on businesses acquisitions. Probably more importantly she accompanied him on many of his business trips, and the parties and events he attended.

She was so grateful to him she just didn't stop to think, didn't question that she was perhaps wasting her brain. She didn't question the fact that she was only being used as eye candy.

She was stunningly beautiful, with exquisite manners to accompany him when he needed it.

As ordered the offices of the University housed across the hall from the Raymond George's Attorney offices were being cleaned. When completed, there would be no trace of any papers or anything that could connect Billings to the University.

There would, however, be a dead University President slumped over on his desk. Blood soaking the carpet from the gun used on his head. On his desk beside him would be a note explaining he didn't want to put his family through a long drawn out investigation. He loved them so much and was very sorry.

A rumor had been put out that the Feds were on to him, and papers were being drawn up to confiscate everything from the offices for his impending arrest.

The rumor was the first the FBI had heard of this, but they went along. The only time they had even heard of the University was when a young student jumped from the building where the University was located, and that was ruled a suicide. The case had been closed, now, of course, it would be reopened. Papers had been left that indicated possible embezzlement.

University President Brook's family would be ruined, as well as countless others. Mr. Billings was satisfied his involvement had been wiped clean. He smiled and collected his coat and briefcase, then headed out the door. His car awaited to take him to JFK.

He leaned back in the luxurious leather seats while sipping champagne.

All and all it had been a good run. He estimated approximately twenty billion from this particular investment during his tenure in New York City. When the young student jumped to his death, Billings saw the writing on the wall. He began wiping out any association with the University. President Brook had gotten careless. Now he paid the price.

As Billings and his beautiful young assistant Carrie fastened their seat belts, awaiting the private jet to take off, the cleaning team was hard at work. The next day, the building that housed the underground computer hacking business was completely destroyed by fire. Faulty wiring was said to be the official cause. Five men and three woman that worked in the building, died in the fire. Billings closed his eyes and thought about the events that had taken place in the past few days.

He had been informed that Mrs. Roberts and her attorney Raymond George were helping one of the students from the University. God only knew what the kid was telling them.

Also, for an entirely different reason, a certain group was hired by the University to kidnap Mrs. Roberts. The hackers had discovered a possible link between her and the raids by NYPD. The idiots didn't have a clue what they were doing. They had no idea what was taking place across the hall from the University at Raymond George's office.

The hired guns had gone off half-cocked. The right hand didn't know what the left hand was doing. He had heard the initial plan was to kill Ms. Roberts, however, he became aware some of the men had gone rogue, had made plans to ransom the woman. The University had no clue, and that was the fatal mistake. Billings could have put a stop to all of it if he had wanted to, but he had already begun to distance himself from the University. He got all the money out and nothing was left that connected him. He no longer cared.

What he did care about was what was about to happen. The kidnapping would bring Senator Jake Freeman into the mix. He would hold nothing back to rescue her. He knew the Senator well, and he had Carrie research Mrs. Roberts. She was the woman with the Senator a few weeks back at the fundraiser he and Carrie attended. Billings realized she was his girlfriend. He had read page six and heard all the negative gossip. He knew it was all bullshit, but it was out there anyway. He liked it that Mr. Senator Perfect was getting a little mud slung at him. He didn't like him, never did, but he was very aware what Jake was capable of.

He had no desire to go up against the Senator. Oh, he knew he could destroy him if he chose, but at what cost? Wasn't worth it. He had warned them, but they didn't listen, now their fate was sealed. They all had to go. There could not be anyone or any evidence left behind pointing in his direction. He had survived and thrived in his businesses by being smart, by taking measures such as this over the years when necessary.

He had warned them, it was their own fault. The car came to a slow stop, and Donald Billings walked toward the awaiting private jet.

Chapter 19

After his meeting, Jake went back to his hotel to take a shower. Just as he finished getting dressed, he heard his cell phone. He smiled when the caller ID read Madison.

"Hi there."

"Uncle Jake, is mom with you?"

He could hear the worry in her voice.

"No babe, she is probably at home. I am on my way over there now."

"I have been trying to reach her for over an hour. She is not answering her phone or text."

"She is probably taking a nap or something."

"Uncle Jake, when my dad died, right before he died, I got this hole in the pit of my stomach. I had to throw up, and that was before I got the call. Uncle Jake, the same thing is happening now, the very same thing, only worse. I can't breathe. Please go find her."

"I am on my way. I will call you as soon as I get there."

He was already out the door and into John's car. Thank goodness he had John on call for the evening. Fear gripped his soul as he unlocked her door. Everything was as they had left it hours ago, but she was not there.

As promised, he called Madison right away.

"I'm on my way over to Duane Reade now. I walked with her there before I left for my meeting. I will call you right back."

He went straight to the checkout counter.

"Yes, she was here. She comes in here a lot, a nice lady so I recognized her, but I didn't see her leave. There is our manager, maybe he will know something."

The store manager realized he was talking to a United State Senator, so he made an extra effort to be helpful. He turned to ask one of the other clerks if she saw Mrs. Roberts.

"Yes, sir, she received a phone call while I was checking her out. I remember because she apologized to me for taking a call while I was helping her. Most people wouldn't think anything about that. Oh, I remember, she said something about having to take the call because it was her attorney."

Jake breathed a sigh of relief. She was at her attorney's office. She probably had her cell on silent if she was meeting with Raymond.

"Thank you, you have been very helpful."

He walked outside as he made the call. He knew her attorney because he helped her brother Jim select Raymond when Nicole moved to New York.

"Hello, this is Senator Freeman, may I speak to Nicole Roberts."

"Certainly, please hold."

Moments later, Raymond answered the phone.

"Good to hear from you Senator."

Jake didn't waste words.

"Raymond, is Nicole there?"

"No, she left a few minutes ago, maybe ten minutes."

Jake could breathe again.

"Great, she is probably on her way home now, thank you."

Before Raymond could engage him in a conversation, Jake hung up and was on his way back to her apartment. He called Madison to reassure her. Jake made himself a drink and set down on the couch to wait. Thank god she was on her way home, yet, after thirty minutes, she still wasn't home. He was in full panic mode again.

"Think man, think."

He called the cab services. Being a Senator made it easier to get information. She was dropped off at Duane Reade. Quickly, he dashed to the store and checked with the cashier again.

"Yes, I checked her out. She left about thirty minutes ago."

Jake thanked her and walked outside. His heart stopped when he saw a Duane Ready sack scattered on the sidewalk. Everything was strewn about, however, the receipt with her signature on it was still in the sack.

John saw Jake run toward the car. He could sense something was wrong. He got out of the car.

"Senator, are you okay?"

"NO!!!!"

He bent over trying to get his breath.

"John, she is gone. Something has happened to Nicole."

He yelled.

"I have to think!"

John assisted him to the car.

Jake called the Commissioner.

"Frank, something has happened to Nicole. I think she had been taken."

A large lump formed in his throat; he couldn't speak.

He handed the phone to John.

"Sir this is John, the Senator's driver. Something has happened to Nicole Roberts."

He explained what little he knew to the Commissioner.

"Get the Senator to headquarter now."

Tire marks were left on the street as John sped around the corner toward Police Headquarters. Jake leaned his head back and closed his eyes, trying to think, trying to breathe.

He thought to himself, "Shit, why did I tell the security team to take the weekend off, just because she was with me."

At that moment Winston's voice slammed in his head.

"Damnit man you promised!"

"God, this is what you meant."

He whispered.

"Winn, I will get her back, God, Winn, I will get her back."

Frank met him at the entrance of his office.

"A car has been sent to pick up Madison and Zack."

Jake pulled out the receipt from Duane Reade and gave it to Frank.

"There is a time stamp on this."

John showed them the plastic bag.

"Just in case your team can pull a print."

John left the room.

Frank continued his update.

"We are already monitoring her credit cards and Jason Thomas is on his way to see if he can track her. She is supposed to keep her designated phone with her

at all times. Not sure she is still on protocol with that. Of course, we don't know yet, but we have to assume this relates to her being on the task force, or it could be a KFR. We just don't know."

"KFR?"

Jake wanted to scream.

"Kidnapped for ransom. We have our phones set up for a trace. We will be getting in sync with Madison and Zack's phones as soon as they get here, we need yours as well."

At that moment, one of the officers came into the room with a note in hand. Frank took it and read it. Jake held his breath.

"There is evidence of a struggle. A piece of a bracelet was found on the street outside Duane Reade. They are bringing it in now."

At that moment, they heard a commotion outside Frank's office. Jake whirled around fast and raced into the hall. Madison raced up to him.

"Uncle Jake, what is happening? Have you found mom?"

He grabbed her and hugged her tight.

"Not yet, baby, but we will, we will."

"Uncle Jake don't protect me. I have to know what is going on. You get that right?"

He pulled her from him and looked straight into her eyes.

"Yes, I do, but we've got to be strong, there is no time to waste."

The two men flanked her and together they walked into the Commissioner's office.

Frank gave Jake a questionable look.

"She has to stay with me. They have to stay."

"Thomas just arrived. He is trying to track her. Right now, I need for you to go with Officer Daniels. As soon as we know anything, we will let you know."

Madison was about to protest, but Jake stopped her.

"Thank you, Commissioner."

He turned Madison toward the door. Once the officer deposited the trio into a waiting room, he left, closing the door behind them. Before Madison could protest, Jake intervened.

"They will keep us informed; I will make sure of that. Right now, I need to find John."

Moments later, he returned with John.

"John has contacted my security team, as well as a special team. They are organizing a search for your mom as we speak."

Madison and Zack looked confused.

"These guys are Special Ops. They are highly trained for search and rescue. Homeland security uses them. They are the best of the best, and we need them."

"Do the police know?"

"No, not yet."

At that moment another officer brought in a package marked evidence.

"Can you identify this piece of jewelry?"

Madison quickly said yes.

"It looks like a piece of the Pandora bracelet I gave mom for Mother's Day."

She turned to Zack. Her whole body shook.

Zack gathered her in his arms and kissed the top of her head.

Chapter 20

She was so cold, her body ached. She tried to move her hands, but they were bound.

"What the hell? Where am I?"

She began to recall what happened. One minute she was walking home from Duane Reade, the next, men came out of the shadows and grabbed her. She struggled to get away but couldn't. They covered her mouth with a cloth, she remembered the smell. It must have been drenched in chloroform or something.

They picked her up, and that's all she could remember. She felt fuzzy in the brain. Nicole shook her head trying to clear her thoughts. Suddenly, she heard voices. Her heart raced with fear. She lay stone still. Angry voices were heading her way.

"Why didn't you kill her? If Omar is right, if she is working with the police, she must die."

Ivan, the man everyone looked to for leadership of their small group said, "True, but you saw her, she is the rich bitch messing around with that billionaire Senator. She must be worth something. I bet he will pay. This is our big opportunity. I say we call him."

"What about the boss, we must inform him, right?"

"I will take care of that, just get today's newspaper, there is one in the van. I will take care of the rest."

They walked up to her and watched as one of the men shoved her in the back with his foot.

"Look at her, she is old, American men are such idiots. I'll take young ones anytime."

The five men laughed as they walked away. That was the moment the will to fight, replaced fright.

"Assholes, I will show you what this old woman can do."

Fortunately, they thought of her as old, therefore, not capable of freeing herself. Back in Memphis, she had taken a survival course with a bunch of her lady friends. She remembered how she and her friends laughed at how crazy it was to be taking the course. Thank god, she had. Now, if she could only remember what the instructor taught them. One of the exercises was on how to free yourself from duct tape. Nicole recalled the instructor binding their hands and feet, then showing them how to get free.

"First, if your hands are bound in front of your body, consider yourselves lucky. Let's try that first."

He showed them how to raise taped hands up above their heads and bring them down as fast as they could. After several tries, she and each of her friends were able to loosen their bindings. Back then, there was a lot of giggling going on, but not now. This time it was life or death and she knew it. She was lucky, for her hands were bound in front.

Over and over, she slammed her hands as hard and fast as she could until she felt the tape began to loosen. Suddenly she heard the men coming her way again. Quickly, she stopped her struggle, and laid down with her back to them just as they had left her. Ivan barked.

"Turn her over."

Today's New York Times was thrown on her and a video was taken. When they were finished, they shoved her again. In the darkness of the room, they didn't notice the duct tape was loose. She heard them discussing how much money they would ask for. She knew in her heart Jake would pay whatever they asked.

As soon as she was sure they were far away, she began again trying to unbind her hands, finally she was free. It only took a few moments to free her legs. Nicole figured she would probably get only one shot at freedom. She began inching her way to the windows. Fortunately, there were stacks of crates near the window. She gingerly began making her way up to the windows. If she could just pry one open. She was sure they were in a warehouse somewhere near the water. She could hear the waves.

Fortunately, the window she tried was not nailed or painted shut. It was crumbling with age, and that made it easier, still it took several attempts and all her strength to pry it wide enough for her to wedge herself through. There was a drop, nothing she could do about that. She closed her eyes and let go of the window ledge.

Nicole hit the cold concrete hard. The pain was almost unbearable, but what could she do.

She muffled her scream, and slowly began making her way across the dock toward the stack of barrels lined up near the water's edge. Everything hurt.

"Find the bitch!"

Nicole was crouched down behind the barrels. It was so cold and damp, her teeth chattered. She picked up a small piece of wood and put it in her mouth to keep herself silent.

They had taken her coat. Her thin blouse was torn. She was bleeding from the jump. Nicole realized she would freeze if she stayed where she was. Frantically she searched for another place. God she was hurting.

Chapter 21

Jake kept looking at his watch. Fifty minutes had passed since John left to coordinate with the Special Forces Group. This group included retired forces from the nation's best Rangers, Navy Seals, etc. Many times, Homeland Security had used this group off book. He glanced at his watch again. Fifty-two minutes passed. The waiting room walls were closing in. He pulled out his cell to call John, when his phone rang.

A disguised voice began talking.

"If you want her back, be prepared to pay. There is a phone in the plant near the front desk. Pick it up and hit dial. Tell no one or she is dead."

Jake smiled at Madison and mouthed he would be right back.

He literally had to make himself walk slowly to the door. Once in the hall, he raced to the front desk nearly knocking the plant over. He reached into the foliage and pulled out the phone, but he didn't punch the button just yet. He has to calm himself. He had to think. He headed back to the hallway and found a vacant room. Quickly he put his phone on silent, then texted John.

"They called me."

Seconds later, John called Jake.

"They had a burner phone in the plant near the front desk. I have it. They want me to call them back right away."

"We have already linked and secured your cell. Put your phone face-down on top of the burner phone, make the call and leave it there for five-seconds. Then remove it but place it to your left against your phone and put them both on speaker, we will be able to hear. Are you ready?"

"Yes."

"Okay, go."

"What took you so long? Why did you leave the front?"

"So, no one could hear. Where is she?"

"A video will be sent to your phone. We will give you two hours to get five million dollars or she is dead."

"I can't get that much that fast, I need more time."

"You are a billionaire Senator, so yes you can. When you have the money, hit dial on this phone. And Senator, screw with us and we will kill her."

The dial tone slammed in his ear. The video popped up on his cell. The air left his lungs as she saw her laying there, bruised and battered and tied up. Her eyes were closed. He barely saw movement.

"God, please."

He jerked when his phone rang, it was John.

"We narrowed the phone to the shipping district."

"Pick me up."

"They figured you would say that. They said to tell you to get the money and stand by. They can't afford for anything to happen to you on their watch. They need all their resources focused on rescuing Nicole."

He screamed into the phone.

"I don't give a fuck about being a Senator. I need to be there."

In the calmest voice he could muster, John stated.

"I think she would want you to take care of her daughter, plus the money needs to be ready."

"Yes, yes, I need to get the money now. But John you must keep me informed. I am about to jump out of my skin."

"I know, Senator, I know."

Quickly, he walked back to where Madison and Luke waited. He spoke quietly, telling the young couple what was happening. He decided not to show them her video. When he finished, he gave Madison a long hug.

"I have to go make arrangements to get the money."

"Uncle Jake, don't we need to tell the Commissioner?"

"Tell me what?"

Jake turned at the sound of the Commissioner's voice. Jake started to say something, but the Commissioner raised his hand to stop him."

"Don't give me any bull shit Jake. I have pulled out all the stops on this. Don't leave anything out. My people are out there, so let me repeat, no bullshit!"

Jake interrupted him.

"They just called me. I need to get five million cash in two hours. I don't have much time."

"Fine, let's do it."

Frank pulled out his phone and punched numbers. It was answered immediately.

"We need five million cash in one hour. Senator Jake Freeman will sign for it."

Frank looked at Jake.

"You are good for it, right?"

Jake nodded yes.

"Good he is with me at one PP. Bring the papers with the money, he can sign for them, make it fifty minutes, no later."

He turned to Jake.

"Now what else are you not telling me?"

"A special ops group have narrowed the location to where she is being held near the loading docks."

"Thanks, we need to coordinate. Give me the contact numbers. I will inform my men."

When the Commissioner turned to leave, Jake followed him into the hall.

He handed Frank the burner phone with the video.

"Did you show?"

"No."

"Good, come with me, we need to get a read on this burner."

Chapter 22

She could see them coming toward her. Nicole knew they would find her if she stayed where she was. She had no choice but to run. The freezing wind blowing off the Hudson was so strong it knocked her sideways as she ran full sped toward a stack of crates close to the water. She squeezed into a narrow opening between two stacks.

"Find her, we have an hour until the Senator shows up. We can take care of the both of them after we get the money. The Boss man said get the money, then go to the shipping dock."

Five men holding machine guns preceded toward the crates. One of them said, "Hell, they will probably give us medals for shooting a Senator. Maybe they should be our next target, ridding Americans of all the idiots running this shit country. We would be heroes."

The men laughed. At that moment, a rough hand grabbed her arm and pulled her from the stacks. He dragged her to where the other men were standing. Once there, he slapped her hard, knocking her down on the asphalt. Fortunately, adrenalin kept the pain at bay.

"Have your fun later, after we get the money."

Now the pain came. It was a pain like she had only known once, pain she couldn't handle. Blood squirted from her nose. Her body was covered with scrapes and bruises, her blouse was toned. They pulled her to her feet and began shoving her toward the warehouse. The leader, Ivan, pulled out his ringing cell and answered. He listened for a moment.

"That was Omar, he said the police are on their way. We have to leave now. The boat is almost at port. Grab our bags and her stuff, we need her alive. Ivan pointed to the drivers. The Boss said to take your men and meet at the dock. We will take our car and get the money, then meet your there. He said to say nothing about the ransom money, not a word, not even to him. He repeated to me twice to tell no one, so don't say a word to him. He said something about other men were there at the docks, whatever that means. I will call the Senator on our way."

Ivan grabbed Nicole's purse and coat from his man and began running toward the car.

"Get her in the car now. Go, Go!"

In a matter of minutes, they were speeding north toward the shipping dock.

Ivan slowed his car to let the two lead cars get far enough ahead so they would not see him turn, then he made a right turn and sped down the graveled road leading to a rundown warehouse. Ivan had already set up the warehouse as his point of operations. He had his team take the young girls they had taken off a ship a few days before. His team of five men were guarding the girls. They had orders to transport these girls to Northern New Jersey to be distributed around the country.

He had to take these girls to the warehouse as ordered so no one would get suspicious. However, once his plan was executed, he would just leave the girls. Ivan was not into sex trafficking. It was a nasty business. And he didn't like being the transporter. This would be the last time he would ever have to do this. When he was far enough away, he would make an anonymous call to 911 about the girls and their location. Hopefully someone would find them.

Ivan had not told his boss, or the other men about the ransom demands he had made. He had been ordered to kill Nicole, but he had other plans. He knew he would have to execute his plan fast, and with precision if he were to get out of this alive. He planned to get the money and run. Ivan was a smart man, who did what he had to do to make money. He had been a hired gun for about six years now. He had built a reputation as being one of the best.

And then he hooked up with these guys. He knew he had made a mistake shortly after the first couple of kills. The money was great, but the people who hired him were brutal. Money was money, but he pretty much knew what was in store for him and the others once they drove to the shipping dock. He had seen what happens to other hired guns, once their usefulness was over. Hell, he had witnessed their elimination.

262

The only reason he figured he was alive today; was they didn't know he had witnessed those men being gunned down. He surmised that this time he would be one of those loose ends. He had no intention of going out that way. This ransom money was his one chance out, and he was going to take it.

Minutes later, the response team surrounded the warehouse where Nicole had been held. They found discarded duct tape, a torn piece of a blouse, and blood spattering's. The forensic team was immediately called to the scene.

"Jake, this is John, we found the warehouse where they had Nicole. She is not here now. They must have just left before we got here. They had to have been tipped off, maybe someone at the Police Headquarters."

Jake braced himself and asked the question.

"Is she alive?"

"There is blood, still, my gut tells me she is alive, and with them. They need her alive to get their money. The team is gathering intel. Jake, we will find her."

Jake hung up the phone. He couldn't speak anymore. He stopped pacing and plopped down on the couch in the reception area. He leaned his head back, and closed his eyes, trying to gather the strength to go back into the room and update Madison. Suddenly, something slammed into Jake stomach. His eyes popped open as he looked around franticly.

"What the ….?"

Once again, he was slammed against the back of the couch. Then he knew.

The words, "Dammit Jake, you promised." Screamed in his mind.

"God, Winn."

Jake could feel Winn's tormented soul blaring into his mind.

"She is almost out of time!"

At that moment, the front door burst open and half a dozen uniformed men entered carrying large black bags entered the building. Jake stood up and walked toward the man holding a clip board.

"Is that the money? Where are the papers to sign?"

All the bags were placed on the floor next to the couch. The other uniforms walked away toward the coffee area, awaiting further orders. Jake scribbled his name as fast as he could and shoved the clip board back to the man.

"The Commissioner has to sign, as well."

The man turned to his officers and said.

"Stay here, I will be right back."

"SHE IS ALMOST OUT OF TIME!" once again hammered into the center of Jake's soul.

He turned around. All the other officers were getting coffee, they had their backs turned. He was alone with the five million dollars. Frantically, he grabbed two of the large bags and raced out the front door onto the street. Once out there, he panicked.

"Winn?"

Seconds later, a black SUV raced up on the sidewalk, screeching to a halt in front of Jake. The window was down. Matt yelled.

"GET IN!"

Jake yanked the back door open, threw the two bags in the back seat and jumped in. Black rubber was left on the streets as the SUV sped away, just as uniforms raced out the front door with their guns drawn.

"Have they found her?"

"No, but they are tracking what appears to be a caravan of SUV'S speeding north toward a loading area for ships. There are two ships in the water nearby. The Coast Guard just spotted one heading toward the docking area. It's coming in dark. Both the Guards and the police are headed there now."

Jake jumped when the burner phone rang.

"Senator, do you have the money?"

"Yes."

He didn't dare tell them he grabbed only two bags. He hoped to god they wouldn't know just how many bags it took to transport five million dollars.

"Good, sit tight we will contact you in thirty minutes."

Ivan quickly hung up the phone. Earlier, he rigged his phone to ping his location so it would appear to be near the loading docks.

If all went exactly as he planned, the police would be engaged in a shootout with the big boss and all his men, while he slipped away with the money.

Ivan intended to have his men watch after the girls, while he and one of his men along with Nicole would meet with the Senator. He planned to meet at an old abandoned gas station not far from where she and the girls were being held. He found the station when he began formulating his plan. There they would exchange her for the money. After the exchange, he would tell his man that the Boss intended to kill all of them when they showed up at the dock. He planned to give his man part of the money to divide with the other men. Ivan had already made up his mind if either his man or the Senator gave him any problem at all, he would kill all of them. He had no time to argue. He knew timing was the most important part of the plan. He had a transport plane waiting for him in a small airport in northern New Jersey. It was his only chance at freedom, and he was taking it.

Jake screamed as he banged the phone on the console, then stopped abruptly, horrified at what he was doing. He could be destroying her only lifeline to him.

Immediately John's team called to tell him they were able to pinpoint the call to be near the docks. Once informed, Matt floored the gas petal hitting close to 90. The police and rescue teams were on their way as well.

The Commissioner rang Jake.

"Jake listen to me. We are on our way. All teams are right behind you. Don't go off halfcocked. We must be smart."

"I know, I know."

The Commissioner hung up. As much as he wanted to blast into the area, he knew better. Suddenly, another slam at the gut, that knocked him hard against the seat. Matt yelled.

"What the hell, are you okay?"

Jake sputtered out.

"I am okay, just please, we have to find her."

"His mind screamed at Winn. Where is she? Help me man!"

Seconds later, Jake barked.

"TURN ON THE NEXT RIGHT."

"But they said…"

"I SAID TURN RIGHT."

"But Senator…"

Jake   pleaded.

"I know, but you have to trust me on this, or get out of the car."

Matt thought for a second, then spoke.

"Senator, do you have a weapon pointed at me? Because if you do, then I have no choice but to do as you say, otherwise I am heading north."

Jake was confused for a half of a second. Then he got it. He quickly placed his hand in his coat pocket and pointed his finger toward Matt.

"Yes, yes I do have a weapon. It is pointed right at you. Take this next right, NOW!"

The SUV tilted on two wheels, barely making the sharp turn. Nothing else was said, until Jake told him to stop on the graveled road. They could see a warehouse up the road. Jake turned to Matt.

"Call John, give him our location. Tell John they must maintain complete silence."

Jake kept his finger inside his pocket pointed at Matt, while he eased out of the car and quietly made his way to the warehouse.

"Stay here and wait for them."

"Fuck! Shit!"

Matt could see his career tanking right before his eyes, as he watched the Senator go it alone into the darkness. Quickly, he phoned John. They were a good fifteen minutes out. A lot could happen in fifteen minutes. He grabbed his sniper rifle and vest from the back and headed toward the Senator. Matt knew he would have to use all his special ops skills to get the Senator and his lady out of this mess.

Stealthy, he made his way up the road. Once he had eyes on the Senator, he positioned himself, and his rifle, then made another call to John.

Jake could see two vehicles parked near the entrance of the structure. That had to be them. He spotted stacks of crates leaning next to the building near a window. There were three stacks that went up about fifteen feet.

Carefully, he began climbing the wobbly crates. Twice the shaky wood began to give way against his weight. Fortunately, he eased to another stack, before the boxes fell.

At last he reached the top of the pile. The window was just inches away, if only he could make it without crashing down the crates. He paused for a second, trying to figure out what was the best move. At that moment, he heard screams from within the building. It was not Nicole but a younger female voice.

"God?"

Then he heard her voice. He almost cried out at the sound but caught himself. He thought he heard scuffling noises.

"Shut up Bitch."

Then a scream as she was being hit. It was Nicole, he was sure of it. They hit her again. Without really thinking, Jake kicked the adjacent piles of crates causing them to tumble. The crash was loud. It did the trick, the men stopped and raced out of the building to see what happened.

It took only seconds for guns to be aimed at Jake, as he slowly descended the pile of crates. He took as much time as he could, praying that John and the team would arrive soon. He whispered to himself.

"Winn."

At that moment, a shooting star flashed across the dark sky. Jake caught his breath, hoping against hope it was a sign from Winn. He turned toward the men and walked with them into the building. He had no time to waste, he had to get Nicole out alive.

"Senator, I told you to sit tight. How did you find this place? I routed the cell phones to the docks."

He paused a moment, then continued.

"Where is the money? Get it now, or she dies."

A gun was raised pointing directly at her.

"Let her go and I will get your money."

"Doesn't work that way. Where is the money, you have ten-seconds to tell us where it is or you both die!"

Jake surmised that while this man came from a different culture, perhaps Russia, he was educated in the states. He spoke perfect English. He also surmised he knew what he was doing, so he couldn't be easily fooled.

"I hid the bags in the ditch near the entrance from the road. My hired guns, not the police are guarding the money. Unless they hear the all clear from me, they will shoot whomever tries to take the money. Look, I don't care about the money, you can have it, I just want Nicole to walk out with me. Seriously man, that is all I care about."

Nicole spoke, at that moment.

"And the girls too, you have to let these girls go."

Jake chimed in.

"Five million dollars will go a long way. You could all start new lives. Just walk away. If for some reason you are caught, I can get you amnesty, after all I am a Senator, and it is my money. I will not press charges. I will tell the authorities that this has all been a misunderstanding, and I am loaning you the money. I will personally guarantee all of you freedom, just let us walk away. I can make this happen."

He quickly pulled out his business card and his pen. He scribbled a note on the back. Look, I wrote and signed an IOU on the back, it's yours. Take it and go before the police get here.

Jake could tell he was making headway with some of the men. Evidently, most of them understood English.

"You have about fifteen minutes tops to get out of here before the police arrive. This is the day of GPS. Don't you get it, there is no exit plan for you guys. Whoever heads up this operation considered you expendable, and I am betting they don't know about the five million. But they do know the police and special teams will be on their way here. Your leaders will make sure all of you are dead before this day is over. It is called tying up loose ends. We have seen the results many times with these leaders. So many bodies left in their wake. I am telling you the truth; you know that don't you? Now is the time to take the money and go."

Jake paused for a moment and looked at each man square in the eyes. A couple of the men questioned Ivan about the money. It was working. The men lowered their guns and began walking toward the front of the building. Jake eased closer to Nicole. Everyone started walking toward the door except for the young girls in the locked cages. Nicole looked at Jake. He knew what was on her mind. She didn't want to leave without the girls, yet, all their chances were much better if she left the building. He didn't have time to explain, so he mouthed.

"Trust me."

Finally, they were at the door. If he could just get her out the door and away from her captors, Matt and the ops team would take care of the rest. The men shoved the two out the door in front of them. They were all walking toward the money. Suddenly, one of the men that had gone ahead turned and raced up to the rest, yelling. Nicole could interpret enough of the words to realize things were falling apart fast. She tried to intervene.

"NO NO, he is not like that. You can trust him."
One of the men grabbed her, while another took the Senator. Ivan yelled.

272

"He is the one that will get us out of here, she is of no use now."

Jake didn't know exactly what they were saying, but he could tell. Two of the men stopped, turned, and aimed their guns at Nicole. Where the amount of herculean strength came from, he would never know, but somehow, he broke free of the men holding him. He ran to the ones aiming their guns at her. He let out a blood curdling scream as he leaped toward them.

"NOOOOOOOOOOO!!!!"

He knocked one gunman down, but the other was able to fire. Jake whirled around in time to see the lead slam into Nicole's body.

"NOOOOOOOOOOOOOOOOOO!!!!"

Jake raced like a wild animal toward the shooter, who tuned toward the Senator to fire. At that exact moment, Matt's sniper's gun rang out instantly stopping the shooter's heart. Fortunately, the force of Matt's bullet made the shooter's bullet propels to the left, hitting Jake in his upper arm, not his heart. Jake fell to the concrete.

At that instant, multiple shots were fired stilling the others. Matt and the special ops cautiously but quickly eased toward the scene where Jake and Nicole lay. Quickly he checked Nicole and Jake. Copious amounts of blood flowed from both their bodies. Jake used all the strength he had left to crawl to Nicole. He gathered her in his arms cradling her saying her name over and over.

Mass Chaos ensued as the police arrived at the scene.

"He has been shot. The Senator has been shot! Get the paramedics down here now!"

The officer reached down to help pull the Senator up.

"NO!"

He screamed.

"Don't touch me!"

"Sir, you have been shot, we need to get you to the hospital."

"NO!"

"She needs help, she needs help!"

Tears swelled up in his eyes. Fear like he had never known clamped down on him. He cradled her closer to him.

"Baby, baby, stay with me, stay with me."

Jake looked up searching.

"John, where is John?"

The big man pushed his way through the sea of blue.

"I am here, Senator, I am here, the paramedics are right behind me."

Jake grabbed John's sleeve and pulled him to him. He whispered in desperation. John nodded and directed the paramedics. Seconds later, a stretcher raced to a stop. Without a pause, they reached pass the Senator, and took charge of Nicole. Another few seconds, they had her on the stretcher as they sprinted across the concrete toward the ambulance. Jake heard one of them say.

"Pulse is weak, breathing's shallow."

274

He watched as paramedics surrounding the rolling bed, frantically working over Nicole's blood-soaked body.

"Winn."

His brain seemed to stop there, for he kept repeating his best friend's name.

As he was lifted into the second ambulance, his eyes were glazed over. He answered no questions, he heard nothing. He just kept repeating the same word.

"Winn."

The paramedics assisting him into the vehicle, just looked at each other.

"At a time like this, the Senator is worried about winning? What a jerk."

Finally, they made it to the hospital. Expert care givers were there. The Senator had been shot. The staff grabbed his gurney and raced toward the emergency room doors. Nicole was rolled in behind him.

"She's crashing."

The paddles were brought out.

"Clear."

"Again."

"Clear."

"Still no pulse."

The Doctor raised the voltage.

"Clear."

This time, there was a slight rhythm registering on the monitor. Quickly the doctors and nurses in the emergency room C raced around the machines doing what they were trained to do. Now, each held their breath waiting for confirmation of a steady heart rate. Emergency room A housed the United State Senator. The hospital's best was sent to attend to his needs. Jake knew the protocol. With his good arm, he grabbed the white coat of the doctor who had begun to examine him.

"Doctor, please go to Nicole. She needs you more than I do."

Dr. Richmond replied.

"She has Doctors attending her. Now let's take a look at your wounds."

"No! Damn it. I know the protocol. You are the best, that is why you are in here with me. Look, I am okay, but she needs help, she needs the best, please go take care of her."

The Doctor just looked at him for a moment, then began again.

"Please, god please, I am begging you man."

Once again, the Doctor just stared at him then said.

"Screw it."

He knew the CEO, CFO and whatever O's would be up his ass, but the Senator was right. While still a gunshot wound, it could be contained. Any one of his team could take care of the Senator. However, the woman next door was close to death. He knew because he was working on her when they pulled him off to attend to Senator Freeman. He nodded to Jake and was off. Quickly he rounded the corner to emergency room C.

"May I join you?"

There seem to be a collective sigh of relief within the confines of machines, doctors and nurses alike.

"One of you go attend the Senator."

His eyes locked on one particular Doctor. She peeled off and headed toward room A. Doctor Richmond stepped closer and began to take charge.

"Get me two CCs of Arrhythmias."

For the next several hours, the team worked on the fragile female lying still on their table. Twice they lost her, twice, they had to use the defibrillators to get her back. So much was wrong. Crushed ribs, severe hypothermia, cuts and abrasions all over her body, not to mention a gunshot wound, through her abdomen. By some miracle the shot missed the important vitals, however, a gunshot was what it was, metal tearing into her, and the loss of blood was a huge factor.

The team finally saw a glimmer of hope. The monitor began to register a slight steadiness in her heart rhythm. Dr. Richmond closed her up. As her heart rate continued to register somewhat steady, he let out a huge sigh of relief. He looked at his team through his tired eyes and smiled slightly.

"Well team, I think we have just witnessed a full-fledged miracle of God's hand guiding us, for we all know there is no way this woman should still be alive. That and how hard she is fighting to live. However, we also know she is not out of the woods yet. She will need round the clock for the next 24 hours."

He looked at the head nurse in attendance.

"Set up a complete minute by minute full chart. When you are finished, bring it to my office. And schedule code blue to be on full alert. God gave us a miracle, let's not let him down."

He started toward the door, then turned back to his team.

"Amazing job everyone."

With that, he left to clean up then headed to room A.

They were too busy to hear the commotions just outside the emergency room entrance. News media had gathered in force, trying to get the latest for their networks. Most of them, could smell it. This was one of those elusive career makers. They were all jostling for position. Suddenly, someone noticed a young couple heading for the entrance. Policemen surrounded the two as they pushed their way through.

Someone shouted.

"That's the daughter."

One reporter clamored close and stuck a mike into Madison's face.

"So, is the story true? Is the Senator your father? Is that why you are here?"

The policeman assisting the couple drew his arm up accidentally hitting the reporter's arm, knocking the mike out of his hand. Quickly they were shuffled inside. There, nurses escorted them into a nearby VIP suite reserved for Presidents, Senators, Celebrities, and other noted people.

"Where is my mother, can I see her, is she okay?"

There was hardly a breath between each question. The designated nurse calmly addressed the couple.

"Hello, my name is Margie Collier, I am the executive nurse for the hospital."

She crossed over to them.

"The Doctors are with her now. As soon as we can, we will inform you of her condition. In the meantime, can we get you coffee, water, or anything?"

Both nodded no.

"Please try to relax. I will check her progress."

Madison paced, and Zack stood.

"The Senator, is he here?"

"The Doctors are with him as well."

Nurse Collier gave a short smile, turned and left.

"I can hardly breathe."

Zack walked over and wrapped his arms gently around his wife. An excruciating two hour passed before anyone spoke to them about her mom's conditioned.

Madison walked to the ICU front desk to try to get some information.

"The Doctors are still with her. We should hear something soon."

"Oh, god, please tell me how my mom is, and where is Uncle Jake."

Tears formed in her eyes.

"Please, tell us."

"As soon as I know, you will know."

At that moment, two nurses and an orderly were steering a gurney occupied by the Senator, heading to ICU. Madison realized who it was and raced to his side.

"Uncle Jake, Uncle Jake!"

He raised his hand slightly motioning for the orderly to stop the gurney.

Jake gave Madison a weak smile. He tried to raise up, instead he began coughing.

His head swam, his heart raced. Quickly the nurse came around to his side to administer oxygen.

"Just close your eyes Senator, take a breath."

After a few moments the room stopped whirling, and his heart slowed, and the nurse removed the mask.

"Uncle Jake, how is mom?"

She took a closer look at Jake.

"Oh my God, Uncle Jake, what happened? Were you shot?"

"I'm okay, and your mother is getting the very best care."

"Was she shot too?"

He had to tell her.

"Yes."

"Oh God, oh God."

"They just told me she came through surgery. I don't know anything more."

"What happened?"

"Your mom was very brave, she fought hard to get away."

"How did you get shot?"

Tears began to stream down his face. His whole body shook.

"I couldn't get to her in time."

Madison placed her hand on his arm, afraid to touch anywhere else. Zack walked over to his wife. They just held each other. Jake closed his eyes.

A moment later, Doctor Richmond walked out into the hall and up to the Senator's gurney. He gave the nurse a strong look of disapproval.

"He needs to be in the recovery room stat. Why have you stopped?"

Madison pleading eyes locked on the doctor.

"How is my mom? Please tell me."

"Mrs. Roberts is stable now. We were able to stop the bleeding and made the necessary repairs. We are going to keep a very close watch on her for the next 24 hours."

He examined Jake with his eyes the entire time he spoke to the young couple.

"Your mom is a very strong woman, with a great will to live, a real fighter, else she wouldn't still be with us. Quite frankly it is a miracle, still she is not out of the woods, but my prognosis for her is guarded but somewhat optimistic."

He turned to Jake.

"Now Senator, we have to wheel you to ICU. I did what you asked, now you need to do what I ask."

With that, the Doctor motioned for the nurse to move his patient.

The next forty-eight hours were touch and go for Nicole. Twice Madison and Zack huddled together as they watched the code blue team race to her mom's room. The two held their breaths until word was sent that she had stabilized. Prayer couldn't be said fast enough. Bargaining pleas to God went on continuously. Fortunately, the VIP waiting room was a two-bedroom hotel suite. On the fourth day, Jake was moved into one of the bedrooms, while Madison and Zack occupied the other. The young couple left to pick up clothes, and take care of the dog, while Jake had John get his things.

One the sixth night, Jake eased out into the open waiting area. So many families gathered awaiting word about the fate of their loved ones. There were no comfortable beds and showers for these people. Moms and dads with little kids in their laps. Others trying to sleep on the hard chairs. He walked down the hall toward the intensive care unit. Jake glanced at his watch; it was 2 am. The lights were dimmed, the critical care unit was quiet. Jake slipped into the area where Nicole's cubical was. There was no one attending her at the moment. As he started in, he noticed a strange glow coming from her room. No one was there, yet....

He watched Nicole raise her left hand as if she was holding someone's hand, but no one was there. He stood frozen as his heart slammed at his chest. This can't be!

"No, Winn, don't take her."

He chocked

"Please, Winston, please, I am begging you man."

Suddenly, there was a sense of calmness filling the room. The glow brightened, then faded. After a few moments, Jake walked into the room, pulled a chair next to her bed, and took her hand, gently caressing her fingers. As he silently sat there, he thought of all the dreams he had experienced over the past year. He thought of why he raced out of the police station like a mad man and how he ended up at that warehouse where Nicole and the girls were being held, a place that was on no ones' GPS. He said a silent prayer thanking God and Winston. Around 5 am, he kissed Nicole's hand and quietly left. For the first time since the ordeal began, he actually slept. It was passed noon when he emerged from the VIP room. As he rounded the corner to the open waiting area, a man came up to him.

"I understand you are the one responsible for our breakfast and now lunch? Thank you, it is much appreciated. Also, thank you for the pillows, blankets, and Aero beds for the kids. It makes it easier for everyone."

Jake smiled and nodded his head.

"This is a hard time for all of us.... This waiting"
The lump in his throat prevented him from continuing.

"I hear you man."

After clearing it with the hospital's CEO, Jake had made arrangements for John's cousin's food truck to deliver breakfast and lunch to the waiting room for the families. Dr. William Shutter, the hospital's CEO said that if they met all the health department regulations and delivered efficiently, set up and took down in the same manner it would be fine. The hospital had its own cafeteria, so this was temporary. Of course, the fact that Jake wrote a big check and handed it to Dr. Shutter helped. As Jake started toward Nicole's intensive care unit, he saw the big man and his entourage walking through the automatic doors. He stopped and waiting for him.

"Frank, good to see you."

The two men shook hands.

"How is Nicole?"

"Holding her own."

"Listen Frank, in all the craziness, I forgot about the burner phone. It was in the plant at your headquarters. Someone knew I had moved to a private room to take that call. I was being watched. Do you think maybe it was someone from your office?"

Frank nodded.

"Actually, it was. His name is Omar. It seems, he had his way with Mrs. Carmichael from the HR department. He talked the poor woman into signing papers as an independent contractor to work on our computers. He hacked into our data base. That is how he found Nicole's name even after we had her information removed. He saw her a couple of times at headquarters, so when one of the computer hackers from their cell, spotted Nicole on video and photos, Omar connected the dots, and Nicole became a target."

Frank smiled.

"It was the time-honored woman scorned scenario. Mrs. Carmichael told us everything when she realized she was being used. We were able to take down a huge cell operation. You should have seen their setup. Jake, they had an arsenal large enough for a small country."

The Commissioner smiled at a couple as they passed, then continued.

"Kids were shipped in to do the trolling. It was quite an operation. You wouldn't believe how badly those boys were treated. Turns my stomach."

"Frank, I am on the Homeland Security Committee, I am afraid I do."

"Nicole's attorney, Raymond George has been helping us with all the legal stuff, with the young man that Nicole helped as well as the other kids involved."

Frank paused for a moment.

"She took a real chance helping that boy. She saved his life, at her peril, however, I think she was probably already a target. That boy was beaten badly, but his friend had it far worse. He couldn't find a way out and took his own life. He was the jumper from that University. We are sure the school administration was involved with this. By odd coincidence, the University was across the hall from Raymond George's office. And even odder, and more damning, the school closed their doors right after Nicole was taken, leaving behind a dead University President. Seems the man, just couldn't live with himself any longer. Confessed all his many sins in a letter left on his desk near his body. A little too wrapped up for me. We are continuing to investigate."

He inched closer to Jake and lowered his voice.

"Jake, that office was scrubbed by professional cleaners, I'm talking Special Ops kind of job. Also, across town, an office and two apartments were cleaned in the same manner. A neighbor was concerned about her young friend that lived in one of the apartments across from her, called it in. This woman said the young lady always told her when she was going out of town. After a few days of not seeing her young friend and spotting four big men coming out of her apartment late one night, she phoned the police. Our men investigated and found nothing. I mean nothing left in the apartment. Fortunately, her neighbor, Mrs. Jefferson knew where the young lady worked. Same thing at the business address, completely cleaned."

He stepped back and continued.

"You won't believe who owned the company where the girl worked. Donald Billings, and you guessed it, his residence was cleaned as well, just like the other places, same M.O. Can't have one of our prominent citizens disappear without a trace, so we have put out a BOLO for both Billings and his assistant, Ms. James. Don't know the connection yet, but I don't believe in coincidences especially this many. Red flags all over the place."

Jake chimed in.

"Well, I have never been a fan of Billings. Always felt a long shower was needed after being around him. Don't like the man."

"I recall him introducing his assistant to us at Madison's gathering. He called her his ward. Didn't seem to ring true at the time."

"We have doubled down on investigating this. Doubled our manpower."

He began walking down the hall, Jake followed. They passed the waiting room where families were surrounding a food table.

"Are you responsible for that?"

Jake just smiled.

"Good man."

Madison and Zack spotted Jake and the Commissioner. Madison walked up.

"Thank you so much for all you did to get my mom back."

"She is a strong, smart lady. The programs she put together are genius. We are in process of implementing one as we speak."

Once Madison left their side, Frank turned to Jake.

"We stopped this group just in time. Not only were they trafficking young girls and boys, they were also planning multiple attacks in our city, much like the ones in Paris. Homeland is all over it. Since you are on the committee, I thought you should know. Unfortunately, we didn't catch the top guy, but we believe it to be

Billings and we are getting closer. We have to be one hundred percent sure of his identity before we proceed."

"Good to hear."

"The UN is partnering with us concerning the young boys that were recruited from small villages in northern Russia. These boys are the ones responsible for the hacking into our systems. It seems they were taken from their homes at a young age. The boys didn't know any better, at least I hope not. Raymond George is helping with the legal stuff."

Frank turned to face Jake.

"Enough of that, Jake were you trying to ruin me, ruin my city. Not a good thing Senator, not a good thing at all."
The Commissioner pointed his finger at Jake's chest.

"I asked you, no ordered you to stay put at HQ. Why didn't you? And how did you know where Nicole was? That place wasn't on our radar."
The Commissioner took a step back.

Jake you have to know if there had been one-second more, one inch more, you would be dead. That man was pulling the trigger. If your snipper hadn't shot him when he did, that bullet would have headed straight to your heart. One second more and..."
Frank demonstrated how close with his fingers.

"This close, Jake, this close."
He lowered his hands and shook his head.

"You of all people should know what it does to a city when a prominent citizen gets shot while visiting. Nicole's Memphis is still in recovery mode, as well as Dallas."

Jake just threw up his hands as if to say I can't explain. But he could, it's just, no one would believe him. He could tell them it was Winston who told him were to go, but most likely he would be carted off the looney farm.

It had been nine days since Nicole was admitted to the hospital, after being shot. Nine days since all the doctors and nurses pulled out all their miracles to keep her alive. On the tenth morning, Doctor Richmond tapped on the door of the suite.

The three held their breath.

"She is awake, weak, but awake."

Everyone let out a loud sigh of relief.

"Madison, would you like to come with me for a minute?"

Tears formed.

"Yes."

Quickly, the two left the room.

"Thank God, thank God."

Zack and Jake just looked at each other. The younger man crossed over to Jake and gave him a manly pat on his back, then preceded to the kitchen. Jake plopped down on the couch unable to move. A few minutes later, Zack offered the Senator a cup of coffee.

They both sat silently for a few minutes. Each man deep in his own thoughts of thankfulness. Madison finally came back into the room. Zack immediately went to her. Through her tears, she told them her mom was alert.

"She knew me, knew my name, knew basically what happened. Jake, she asked if you were all right? Then she smiled at me, went back to sleep.

Dr. Richmond said her clarity was a very good sign."

She hugged her husband tighter, unable to speak anymore. Since Jake was not family, he was not supposed to visit with Nicole. It was protocol, however, at night, the nurses quietly ignored him as he made his way to her cubical. Being a Senior certainly helped. Finally, she made enough progress to be allowed into an ICU private room. The three of them took turns staying with her.

A routine was established. Things were getting back to normal in this highly abnormal circumstance. It had been over a month since he had been back to Washington, however, he had no intentions of leaving Nicole.

Madison and Zack went to their workplaces during the day, and Jake did his Senatorial duties via internet and phone. With Amanda's help, Jake hired a top designer to coordinate the move into Nicole's new home. Madison helped with everything when she could. Jake had plenty of time to think, while he sat in the chair next to Nicole's bed. He did a lot of soul searching.

Almost losing Nicole, almost losing himself, put things into prospective. One thing he knew for sure. He could not go back to business as usual. His heart was no longer in it. He just didn't want to waste his time going through the motions like he knew in his heart he had been doing for the past year or so.

It wasn't fair to his constituents; it wasn't fair to him. He put his move to New York City in motion. He formally handed in his resignation to the Senate, with the promise to help the new appointee adjust. He was very happy when his good friend Jason Vickers was named interim appointee for the position. He was a good man; he would work hard for Tennessee.

Amanda agreed to make the move to New York. A huge raise helped encourage her to uproot her family. Jake provided a home in the Forest Hills area for her. John was already on board. It was a start.

Chapter 23

It had been almost two months since Nicole and Jake were rushed to the hospital. At last, it was time to go home. Both Madison and Jake held their breaths when they opened the door to Nicole's new home and wheeled her inside.

"Oh my God! I love it, I love it. Sweetie, it is so beautiful."

Happy tears rolled down her face.

"I love you all so much."

She grabbed Jake arm and squeezed it.

Madison interjected.

"Jake is the one, he did so much to coordinate everything."

"Well, full disclosure Amanda is the one that coordinated everything for the move. Then Madison and the designer took over."

Nicole laughed.

"One day soon, I want to meet this assistant of yours."

It was too soon to tell her his plans. That would come later. Now she was home. Her new home, and she was happy. For the next several days, Jake fussed over Nicole. They were establishing a brand-new relationship. Jake was no longer unsure how Nicole felt, for she had told him, had shown him. She asked him not to buy an apartment, instead, she wanted him to move in with her. They were a couple forging a life together.

During the day, they made plans about the new foundation they were creating. At night, he laid in bed with his arms around her, while she slept. Since the shooting, Jake spent much of the wee hours just staring at her and thanking God and Winn for saving her life.

The foundation was coming along nicely. Nicole had agreed to become partners with him. He had just completed negotiations to buy the building that Nicole's condo was located in. The top four floors would be dedicated to their businesses, and the foundation.

He made the seven thousand square foot space on the top floor his home. He felt it best. One thing for sure, he included Nicole on all the plans for the foundation. They were developing new feelings of respect, love and trust for each other. He was learning so much about women and their amazing abilities because now he paid attention, really paid attention. If only more of his gender would realize the capabilities of the fairer sex, the world would be so much better off.

Nicole stood in the doorway and watched Jake discuss with the contractor what he wanted done to his apartment, as well as the foundation offices. As she watched, she thought about how close she had come to losing her life, and how hard she had fought to get it back. She spent many sleepless nights thinking about that one night she had been so willing to throw her life away, and then to have to fight so hard to get it back, when someone else tried to take it. Over and over again Nicole thanked God and asked for forgiveness.

She felt such gratefulness to him for not giving up on her. She also talked to Winn everyday about all the private things that she couldn't verbalize with anyone else. She had decided she would make an appointment with a therapist. She had finally let go of all the guilt about his death. She couldn't tell anyone just yet, but in her heart, she knew he saved her when she tried to take her own life, and he was there beside her as she fought so hard to live. She felt his presence, felt his hand holding hers. Jake interrupted her thoughts.

"Nic, what do you think about moving this wall over here? Do you think it will give us a better flow in the office area?"

A few weeks later, Jake picked Nic up to take her for a drive. She had not been out of the building except for doctor appointments and was getting a bit stir crazy. He smiled as he drove through the Lincoln Tunnel toward New Jersey. They headed south on interstate 95. They talked about their new business. Both were excited about all the possibilities. He watched the spark in her eyes as she talked about her ideas for the foundation. They held hands as he drove I-95 South toward a town called Colts Neck. They had been driving for over an hour, when Jake suggested they stop to get a bite. He turned into the Blue Meadows Restaurant parking lot.

It was all planned. The hostess greeted the couple and led them to their table. At first, she didn't see Madison and Zack when they entered the big room, then she did. Oh, how nice they were all going to eat together.

She hadn't yet realized the restaurant was empty except for them. A half dozen tables were all decorated for a party. Lighted candles and huge floral arrangements surrounded the area creating a special atmosphere.

Moments later, John and his family, along with Amanda and her family came into the room. Matt was there as well.

Jake introduced everyone. Nicole was especially glad to meet Amanda.

"I am so happy to finally have the opportunity to meet you. I think I have so much to thank you for."

About fifteen minutes of small talk, every one began to gather around just standing smiling broadly at her. It was weird.

"Jake what is going on?"

At that moment, the door of the restaurant opened. A really good-looking man in his sixties, wearing jeans, and a worn leather jacket entered. Two men in suits looking much like bodyguards accompanied him. One of the men carried a guitar case. They walked over to Nicole and the Senator.

At first Nicole, didn't get it. Then she did. Nicole covered her mouth as she giggled like a starry-eyed teenager.

"HOLY CRAP SHIT!"

THE END

Made in the USA
Columbia, SC
19 February 2020